MASTIFFS, MYSTERY, AND MURDER

D1522676

MASTIFFS, MYSTERY, AND MURDER

A DOG DETECTIVE SERIES

SANDRA BAUBLITZ

The author wishes to thank:
Lisa Shea, for her advice and support.
S.A. Soule of SwoonWorthy Book Covers, for her outstanding covers and patient help.
Her mother, Goldie Baublitz, for her encouragement and support.
And Clarissa and Paw's fans whose support keeps these stories alive.

"Dog Rule #1: Always protect your owner."

— THE DOG DETECTIVE

CHAPTER 1

*R*ing!

The doorbell startled me from my comfortable routine of collecting Paw's toys. My Saint Bernard bolted past me to the door, tail waving in wild abandon.

"Woof! Woof!"

Who could be at the door? I wasn't expecting anyone, but clearly, Paw knew who it was. I dumped my armful of toys on a nearby chair, strode to the door, and peeped through the small windowpane set in the door. Bruce Sever stood on the other side, wearing a huge grin.

I pulled open the door. "Hey, sweetheart, I thought you were in Chambersville on that case of the dead accountant."

Bruce, six feet tall with dark brown hair and warm brown eyes, stepped forward, saying, "I missed you," then enveloped me in a bear hug and kissed me.

"Woof!" Paw wedged his head between our bodies, forcing us apart.

Laughing, Bruce knelt, ruffling Paw's fur. "Hello, big guy."

Closing the door, I gestured Bruce into the living room, where he settled on the sofa. "Can I get you something to drink?"

Paw, AKA Paudius Pernivious, followed us, then flopped down over Bruce's feet.

Bruce grunted as two hundred pounds of dog landed on his feet. "Soda, if you have it."

I walked into the kitchen and retrieved Bruce's favorite brand of soda from my well-stocked fridge. I returned to the living room and popped open the can top before handing him his drink. "How'd your case go?"

"I'm still working on it. I've never met a man as hated as Lyon Connors, and yet, I've cleared most of my suspects for his murder."

"If he was that hated, wouldn't it be easy to find out who killed him?"

"That was my opinion, too, until I delved deeper into the case. Connors's neighbors, co-workers, and former friends hated the man. The police ruled his death as a heart attack. His sister, who hired me, is the only one who cares that he's dead, believing her brother was murdered."

"Was he murdered?"

"The toxicology report won't be back for several weeks, but in my gut, yeah, I'm sure he was poisoned."

"Didn't he have any friends?"

"A few and they're all connected to the dog shows Connors competed in. Of course, he has plenty of enemies from those same shows." Bruce ran his hands through his hair, then took a gulp of his soda. "Clarissa, the shows are my only lead, that's why I need your help. I need to borrow Paw."

At the mention of his name, Paw tilted his head to the side and looked up at Bruce.

"Why?"

"Before his death, Lyon Connors had entered a dog show scheduled for this weekend in Dockers. I'm entering the show too."

"Wait! You think someone at a dog show killed Connors?"

Bruce nodded before gulping more soda. "Connors got in a fistfight with another contestant at his last show, claiming the guy tried to harm his dog. It's the only lead I have."

"Bruce, why would anyone kill over a dog show, let alone hunt the person down later?"

"I don't know, but the contestant he had the altercation with will be there. Maybe it is a false lead, but I have to try."

"Can't you just observe?"

"No. I need to be in the middle of everything, so I've called in some favors to get a spot in the show. Clarissa," he implored, "I need a dog for the show and Paw is my best bet. Please let me take him to the show."

I crossed my arms, ready to refuse him. I wasn't comfortable volunteering Paw for this, and I doubted he would even behave. Dog-show dogs always appeared pampered and well-trained. They understood the routine of a show. Paw was spoiled, by me, and for the most part, got to do things his way. I trusted Bruce, but I wasn't sure if he could handle Paw. I didn't want to send my pet into danger although Paw had proven he could handle himself in dangerous situations in the past.

"Can you assure me of Paw's safety?"

"Yes. I plan to keep a low-profile. I'll avoid open confrontation and any evidence I find I'll turn over to the police." He sighed and wiped his hand down his face. "The truth is it's been a long time since I had a dog, but Paw and I will get along fine."

I suppressed my urge to laugh. Paw would do what he wanted to do, not what Bruce wanted. "Why don't I go with you and help you investigate?"

Bruce shook his head. "No." Before I could protest, he said, "I know you can handle yourself, but I don't want you in danger. I promise to keep Paw safe."

I humphed. "I'll let you go with Paw, on one condition: I get to come to the dog show to observe." I raised my hand before Bruce could protest, saying, "I promise to keep away from you and Paw, so no one suspects we are together."

"Deal." Bruce stood up, motioning to Paw. "I need to take him with me now since the show starts tomorrow."

I gathered up Paw's things for a road trip and walked out to Bruce's car with Paw beside me.

Bruce opened the car door, motioning for Paw to get in.

He jumped in the back seat, eager for a ride.

I hated to see Paw so willing to go with Bruce as I considered him my loyal companion.

Bruce put Paw's things on the floor in the back seat, shut the door, wrapped his arms around me, and gave me another kiss. "Don't worry. I will keep Paw safe."

Bruce stepped back, walked around to his side of the car, and opened his door.

Paw had been observing us with his head tilted to the side. When he realized I wasn't going, too, he became agitated and howled, loud and long.

Bruce spoke to him in a soft tone, "Easy, boy, we're just going for a ride." But as Bruce went to get in the car, Paw jumped over the back seat and pushed through the door.

Bruce tried to catch Paw, who ran to the other side of the car.

Bruce switched directions, planning to catch Paw as he continued around the car, but Paw switched directions too.

After several minutes of the chase, Bruce ended up lying on the ground, exhausted from running around in circles.

He huffed. "Change of plans. We'll all go to the dog show. I'll work out a cover story for you being with us."

Paw waved his tail in triumph as I smiled in victory.

I collected my things, loading two suitcases with casual clothes and a few toiletries.

Bruce loaded my bags into the trunk of his car, handed me in, and we set off for Dockers.

As he drove, Bruce explained, "We'll pose as husband and wife – newlyweds. I have hotel reservations under an alias."

"Sounds reasonable. Do you have the supplies we need to show Paw?"

"What supplies?"

"Bruce, if Paw is competing, he needs to have the dog paraphernalia to appear as a contestant. Combs, brushes, styling products, that sort of thing."

Bruce raised an eyebrow. "Doesn't he have stuff you bought him?"

I snorted. "No, he does not. I've never been to a dog show, but even I know they style and groom the dogs for the ring. Paw has minimal grooming supplies. He's more of a rough and tumble kind of dog."

"We'll stop at the next pet store we find."

We found one a few miles later, went in, and purchased what I guessed we needed.

I whispered to Bruce. "I hope we don't appear like amateurs at the show."

Of course, my bigger concern was how Paw would do at the show.

We arrived in Dockers around 4 PM and checked into our hotel, The Haliburton. It was a lovely multi-story hotel with a welcoming front entrance. Colorful potted mums in oranges and reds flanked the entrance while crystal-clear glass front doors had the name – The Haliburton – stenciled on each of the double doors. A doorman dressed in a Haliburton uniform ushered us into the hotel.

The front desk clerk asked, "Will you be keeping your dog with you?"

I hadn't considered that the hotel allowed this. "Yes. We will." Paw loved being near me, and he wouldn't tolerate sitting in a cage in the arena.

A bellhop escorted us to our room which had a small sitting area and a queen-size bed.

The bellhop handed Bruce the room key. "Room service is available around the clock." He gestured to a small table. "The hotel has provided complimentary welcome baskets that include treats for our doggie guests."

Bruce tipped the bellhop, ushering him from our room with a "Thank you."

I took in the décor of our room - cream-colored walls with blue curtains, carpeting, and bedspread. "Nice place."

Paw jumped up and settled on the bed.

Bruce scanned the room. "I booked one of the nicer rooms, and we are next door to Gerald Hoffman, the guy I am investigating. He's the one Lyon had the fight with at the last show. Several of the other contestants are on this floor, too. I requested this room to observe them."

"Makes sense."

By now, I was worried about the sleeping arrangements. It hadn't crossed my mind until we got into the room, but there was only one bed.

Bruce said, "I'll sleep on the couch."

I smiled, thinking how we had been dating but had yet to reach the point where we were that close. "Why don't I sleep on the couch? I'm smaller and will fit better on it. Your long legs are going to hang over the side and hurt your back."

"Sounds like something a wife would say."

"No, a wife would tell you to sleep on the couch when she was mad at you."

He laughed. "True, but I have another motive, whoever sleeps in the bed will sleep with Paw. I'm not ready to share a bed with a huge Saint Bernard."

Now I was the one to laugh.

Bruce motioned to the door. "How about we go check out the arena and dog prep areas? Besides, we need to unload his stuff from the car."

"Good idea." I walked to the bed and gave Paw a hug goodbye.

He was content, asleep on the bed, and only cracked open an eye as we left.

The show was in the events hall, a huge room used for a

variety of programs and events. I was surprised the hotel could accommodate such a space.

One of the staff explained the procedures as he guided us to our designated stall. "There are separate rings for the judges to observe the different categories of dogs. The show will run on Saturday and Sunday with Saturday scheduled for the preliminary judging and Sunday for the final group and Best in Show competitions. We use the American Kennel Association standards of breeds to categorize the dogs. Each category will have a winner and runner-up. Each dog who wins their group will compete for this coveted title. The arena will have three judges working at one time. They each have their support staff who will keep the dogs and their owners moving."

The guide stopped at a small cubicle. "This is your stall."

Temporary half-walls enclosed the ten-by-ten-foot space, leaving part of one side open for a doorway.

The guide continued, "You will need a crate to cage your dog, in the case of emergency."

Bruce crossed his arms. "Emergency?"

The guide nodded. "It is a security measure. If, for example, a dog gets loose in the hall, an announcement will inform you to cage your dog. It ensures against dog fights, or a pack of dogs running through the hall. Besides, your dog needs to be in a cage if you leave him alone in the stall."

I smiled at the guide. "Thank you for your help."

"You are welcome," he said, before walking away.

My shoulders slumped. "We don't have a cage. I've never put Paw in a cage, and I don't intend to start. Besides, I doubt Paw will cooperate if we tried to get him in one."

Bruce uncrossed his arms and hugged me. "I'll go buy one for appearances. Remember that pet store we passed as we came into town. I'll get one there once we unload Paw's stuff."

"Get an extra-large one. Paw won't want to go into one, but we best be prepared."

I walked with Bruce to the car, and in two trips we had all of Paw's supplies in his stall.

While Bruce left to get the cage, I set up our supplies. Bruce had pre-registered, but a staff member came around with more paperwork to fill out. I hunched over the papers trying to describe Paw's "heritage."

A voice behind me said, "Do you need help with the paperwork?"

I looked up to see a tall, late-middle-aged woman smiling at me, her graying blonde hair cut short and curly. A Pomeranian, wearing a black and gold bow, cuddled in her arms.

"Thank you for the offer, but I'll manage on my own. I'm uncertain of my dog's ancestry as Paw was a gift from my husband's late aunt."

The woman sniffed, "Paw?"

"Yes. His full name is Paudius Pernivious, but I call

him Paw. I must admit he got the name because he loves to dig in the garden. He's a purebred Saint Bernard."

"Oh, that's good, dear. You wouldn't guess who is allowed in these shows sometimes. This show is about the best of the best in the dog world. Bitsy here is a pure-bred Pomeranian. She's won many shows, and she will win this one if I prepare her well. I can't see competing against common dogs."

I gulped at her statement. In my book, all dogs were special. Paw's a purebred, but most of all, he is just a lovable companion. However, I was sure Bruce wouldn't appreciate me arguing with the competition.

I brushed aside my insecurities. "Bitsy is beautiful. I must admit this is my first show. My husband is the one wanting to show our Saint Bernard. I'm just learning how to show our dog."

There - let Bruce deal with it.

"Oh, don't worry, dear. You will learn, and then you will live and breathe dog shows. I'm sure your Saint Bernard will do well, but it takes a while to get the hang of things."

She turned around and walked off with her Pomeranian.

I breathed a sigh of relief. I wondered if all show owners were like her.

A deep chuckle sounded behind me, and I turned around to see a tall man with salt and pepper hair standing at the entrance to my stall. Beside him stood an adorable tan and white bulldog with drooping jowls.

He chuckled again. "I see you have met Dorothy. I suppose you are worried that we are all like her, but we're not. Dorothy can be a dear, but some of her opinions are extreme. Her late husband was the same way. The man would get into verbal fights if someone else won a ribbon ahead of him. There are a few others like that, but most of us just love dogs and want the best of the breeds to do well."

He extended his hand. "Guess it would be polite to introduce myself. Jed Gray."

We shook, my hand clamped in a firm grasp.

I opened my mouth to introduce myself, "Clarissa," but I'd forgotten the last name Bruce had given us.

He motioned to the bulldog wearing a dark blue collar who sat beside him. "This here is Tucker Attison, the third, or Tuck, for short."

I knelt next to Tucker, patting his back. "Hello. You are one fine looking fellow, Tuck. I'm sure you will win those judges over tomorrow."

Mr. Gray beamed at me. "Now see, you, young lady, are what I call a true dog person. You treated Tuck like he was an intelligent creature."

"That's because I believe he is, as are all animals."

He smiled. "A wise and kind outlook. You'll do fine in this show. Who is your entry?"

"Oh, my goodness, I forgot to mention Paw. Paw is short for Paudius Pernivious, my Saint Bernard. I guess you can guess how he got his nickname."

"Ha, ha, ha. A digger, right? I bet he can move a mountain of dirt."

I smiled and nodded.

He urged Tuck to stand up with a gentle tug on dog's collar. "I look forward to meeting the fine gentleman. I best get Tuck here settled in for the evening. It was nice meeting you, Miss Clarissa. See you tomorrow."

I waved to them both as they headed to the main entrance connecting the event hall to the hotel.

Studying the paperwork for the show, I sighed. It would take me forever to fill them out. Delaying the inevitable, I set aside the paperwork and strolled through the exhibition hall.

The stalls were set up, and dog owners, who had arrived with a large array of dog-related paraphernalia, occupied them. A few dogs were being groomed. Many owners smiled and nodded at me while others were too engrossed in their grooming tasks to notice anyone walking by.

I had stopped by one stall containing a Chihuahua and her pups. A sign posted on their cage stated the pups were for sale. They were adorable little creatures. All I could think was that Paw's paw was bigger than these little guys.

I was so engrossed in the pups that I failed to see the approaching hotel employee until she stopped next to me.

"Miss? Are you the guest in Room 223?"

"Yes." *Had something happened to Paw?*

"We need you to quiet your dog as he's been barking and whining non-stop for the last half hour. Several guests have complained. We have offered the privilege to the entrants to keep their pets with them provided the pets cause no disturbance. You need to abide by our noise rules."

Chagrined, I apologized, "Sorry. I'll take care of it."

CHAPTER 2

*J*took the elevator to my floor and heard him barking as soon as the doors opened. I hurried to my room and let myself in. Paw stopped barking as soon as I stepped into the room.

"Sorry, boy. I guess I was gone too long. How about we take a walk?" Paw wagged his tail enthusiastically.

I snapped on his leash and picked up the pooper scooper items in case I needed them. We descended the stairs to the lobby, exiting through a side door to the dog park provided by the hotel.

It was a lovely evening, and several other owners were taking advantage of the park. I saw a Maltese and his sprightly female owner talking to a tall and handsome man with a mastiff. Both dogs were beautiful. Paw wanted to visit with every dog in the park, but I restrained him. I wasn't sure how social the other owners wanted to be with their dogs as these were show dogs. Would their owners welcome Paw's exuberant attention?

Paw and I walked around the perimeter of the park. It was a beautiful area with lush green grass, a few healthy shrubs placed here and there, and park benches that looked comfortable. A small wooded area backed the park and squirrels were playing around the base of the trees. I had to haul on the leash because Paw wanted to lunge after them. We made it past the trees, passing the Maltese and mastiff when their owners' conversation caught my attention.

The woman with the Maltese spoke, "Lyon took these shows too seriously. He stressed too much. Probably did his heart in." She was short with auburn hair and dressed in a rose-colored dress suit. I inhaled her perfume which turned my stomach. Her Maltese draped contentedly over her arms. The dog's white coat gleamed.

The mastiff's owner growled, "Wouldn't be surprised if someone killed him." His dog stood by his feet, guarding his master. His tan fur and black face were beautiful. His master wore a scowl.

The Maltese woman looked at him sharply. "What do you mean?"

"Lyon was too competitive. He didn't play fair, either. He cheated somehow at the last show. You know he always found fault with competing dogs to get them disqualified. How could Dorothy stay friends with him?"

The Maltese woman whispered to him, "Be careful

MASTIFFS, MYSTERY, AND MURDER

what you say. People are listening." She glanced around, stopping when she saw me.

I gave a tentative smile and continued walking with Paw, moving out of hearing range.

Paw and I walked until he finished his business then we headed back to our hotel room.

We met Bruce, carrying a grocery bag, in the hallway outside our room. "There you are. I wondered what happened to you."

Delicious smells wafted from the bag.

Paw eagerly sniffed it.

"Paw and I took a walk. He was barking nonstop, and the hotel staff requested I shut him up. I thought a walk would help both of us to relax."

I, too, was curious about the contents of the bag. I tried standing on tiptoes and peeking, but Bruce was taller than me so I couldn't get a good look.

"No peeking." He grinned as he opened the door, ushered Paw and me inside then closed it.

He set the bag on the sitting area's small, round table, suitable for a quick meal. The table would provide enough room for me to write. I had a golden opportunity to write about dogs and dog shows at this event. As a freelance writer, I could use all the new ideas I could find.

Paw stood up to the table, eagerly nudging the bag with his nose.

"No!" Bruce and I commanded in unison. He got down but gave us a wounded expression. I had spoiled

Paw dreadfully. My vet had admonished me not to give him people food unless it was part of a vet-designed diet. She was right, but Paw could look so adorable that I often slipped him a bite or two of my food. Fortunately, he hadn't gained too much weight. A Saint Bernard is a large dog, and Paw was no exception. An extra pound didn't show on him.

Bruce opened the bag. "Figured we'd eat here tonight and discuss how we'll handle the show and investigation."

"Sounds good to me. Did you get the cage?"

"Yes." Bruce set out the food. Burgers and fries weren't the healthiest, but they sure smelled good.

Paw pushed his nose up to the table again, eager for food.

I pulled him back. "No!"

Bruce tipped his head toward Paw. "I bought an extra burger if you want to give him some."

"I shouldn't." But Paw knew I would cave in and give him some.

He gave me his poor starving puppy stare.

I sighed, pulled out the burger, wiped off the condiments, and gave it to him.

Bruce just laughed and started to eat his burger. "The cage is huge. It takes up most of the room in his stall. I can't see him being willing to get in it. It's heavy and awkward to move too. Fortunately, I had help."

"Who helped you? Do they have staff for that?"

"No staff that I saw. One of our fellow entrants helped me. A guy by the name of Matt Monroe. Nice guy.

Apparently, his aunt shows her dog, but she broke her hip, and he's here showing her dog for her. Chihuahuas. I didn't get much more info out of him, but I'll investigate tomorrow. What happened while I was gone? Did you find out anything?"

"I met some of the other entrants." I described Dorothy, Jed Gray, and the conversation I overheard in the park. "They mentioned the name Lyon. I doubt there are two Lyons in the show so it must have been Lyon Connors. From their conversation, it sounds like Lyon wasn't well-liked."

Bruce finished his fries. "We'll start there and ask around tomorrow about Lyon. Get a sense of their reactions."

"No. You may have time to ask questions, but I somehow have to figure out how to get Paw to behave for the judging. Quite honestly, I am nervous. I have no clue what goes on in a dog show let alone how I am going to convince Paw to do it."

"I'm way ahead of you." Bruce handed me a small book titled, *How to Win at Dog Shows*. "Read that. It should give you some pointers. In fact, skip to the part about showing a dog in the ring, and we'll practice with Paw."

"Do you expect Paw to go far in this show?" I had assumed Bruce wanted Paw there to prove we were part of the dog show. Now I wondered if I was wrong.

"It depends on how well my investigation goes. We may need Paw to get to the final round."

I laughed. I couldn't help it.

Bruce frowned. "What's so funny?"

"Bruce, Paw isn't trained. He does what he wants when he wants. I doubt he will make it through the first round of judging. Sitting still and being observed is not his forte. He's more likely to drool on the judges and lick their faces than listen to a command."

I shook my head sadly. "I'm nervous how we'll do in the ring. I've no experience showing."

Bruce grasped my hand. "You and Paw can win. We'll practice tonight. The book has advice for each stage of judging. We'll practice with Paw until he gets it. I promise."

"What about the investigation? I thought you wanted to concentrate on that this evening?"

"Paw doing well is an important part of that. I can power up the investigation tomorrow morning. Besides, how long could it take to get Paw ready tonight?"

Four hours later Bruce had his answer. We had finally given up for the night in exhaustion. Paw hated standing in place patiently for the "judge" (i.e. Bruce) to examine his form. He would fidget, bark, or vigorously wag his tail. He did better at the promenade to see his form, but I wasn't overconfident.

Yawning, I said, "I need sleep. Let's finish in the morning."

Bruce took the settee while I took the bed with Paw.

Paw and I slept soundly. I doubt Bruce did since the settee was too short for a tall man to sleep on comfortably.

I woke early the next morning by Paw jumping off the bed.

Bruce stretched the kinks out of his back from sleeping on the settee.

I showered first then took Paw for a walk.

We weren't the only ones up early. Hotel employees bustled back and forth in preparation for the show which began at nine a.m.

In the dog park, several show participants hurried through their morning constitutionals. No one seemed inclined to stop and talk.

I suppose I wasn't the only one nervous about the show.

Paw finished his business, and we returned to our room to prepare for the day ahead.

Bruce had showered and dressed. He had ordered room service which arrived shortly after Paw and I returned. We ate a quick breakfast of eggs and bacon while I finished Paw's paperwork with Bruce's help.

Bruce grasped the papers. "I'll hand it in for you. Then we'll take a walk around the exhibition to get Paw used to it. Plus, I can observe everyone and find the guy I suspect had something to do with Lyon's death."

"All right. That's something I remember about the conversation I overheard. Neither person mentioned murder. That could be helpful if this guy lets something slip when you talk to him."

"Good point."

I snapped on Paw's leash. He had eaten his dog food plus bites of eggs and bacon, so he was ready for adventure.

We rode the elevator to the lobby then went into the events hall. Paw and I waited for Bruce to hand in Paw's paperwork then we strolled through the exhibition hall. Nearly everyone seemed to be busily in motion. People were grooming their dogs, or carrying filled water bowls, or beseeching their dogs to eat breakfast.

Paw took it in stride. His only complaint was that I didn't let him go and greet the other dogs.

A young man with light brown hair and hazel eyes stood in the Chihuahua stall I visited last night. Of medium height, he was dressed in jeans and a blue short-sleeve knit shirt. I guessed him to be close to my age.

He greeted us as we strolled up to his stall. "Hello, there. Did you get settled in okay?"

"Yeah, we did." Bruce extended his hand. "Thanks again for your help."

They shook hands as Bruce said to me, "This is the guy I told you about, the one who helped with Paw's cage. This is my wife, Clarissa. Honey, meet Matt Monroe."

"Nice to meet you and thank you for your help."

Matt shook my hand then smiled at Paw who was sniffing at the female Chihuahua. "What a beautiful dog.

He must be who the cage is for, though I can't imagine he will like it."

Matt bent down to pat Paw, but first, he glanced up at me to make sure it was okay.

I nodded, but Paw had already stuck his head under Matt's hand, rolling his eyes in delight.

The Chihuahua yipped for attention. She was so tiny but wore her red collar proudly. Her brown eyes radiated intelligence, and soft, tan fur covered her body.

I crooned to her, "You are adorable."

Matt stood up. "Her name is Lila." He shrugged. "At least, that's what we call her. Her official name is too long to use. Showing dogs is my aunt's passion, but she broke her hip, so I'm helping her out."

I scratched Paw's ears. "I'm nervous as I'm new to showing."

"You'll do fine. Paw is the perfect Saint Bernard, and that goes a long way toward the judging."

I smiled, thinking that his behavior might not go over with the judges.

"Have fun." Matt's voice turned cold. "Some here take things way too seriously."

It was the perfect opening. "I overheard two entrants talking about a guy who died who competed at any cost. They said his name was Lyon."

Matt scowled. "Lyon's dead? Yeah, he was an aggressive competitor and a real ass. Sounds terrible, but I can't say that I'm sorry he's dead." He looked at his watch. "I've got to go. Just remembered someone I have to call."

He gently placed Lila in the cage with her puppies then hurried out of his stall. "Good luck with the show," he called over his shoulder.

Bruce watched Matt walk away, saying, "He sure was in a hurry."

"Do you think he didn't know about Lyon's death?"

"Hard to tell. I'll follow him and see where he goes. Then I'll see if I can find Gerald Hoffman, the guy I suspect of Connors's death."

Judging was in three hours. I walked to our stall where I planned to give Paw a fresh grooming, hoping it would calm him and me. As I filtered back through the rapidly filling hall, I heard a familiar voice. I let out a sigh of relief. Off to my left, I saw red-haired, green-eyed Shelbee Van Vight talking to a woman with a dachshund dressed in a red sweater. Shelbee was one of my best friends as well as a pet sitter. She would be able to help me prepare for this show.

Shelbee was deep in conversation with the dachshund's owner when Paw and I walked up to them. The woman smiled at us, hugging her dachshund a little closer to her. It was a beautiful dog with deep brown fur highlighted with reddish hues complemented by its red sweater. Dark liquid-brown eyes looked at me curiously. The dachshund didn't seem disturbed by Paw's presence.

Paw sat at my feet and tilted his head to watch the small dog.

Shelbee turned, her eyes widened when she saw me. She smiled, returning to her conversation.

"Don't worry, Patricia. Pablo will be fine in the show. I've given him a massage that should help keep his back limber and in good form. Let him rest quietly until his turn in the ring."

The woman looked skeptical.

"I understand," Shelbee said, "that it's going to get noisy in here soon, but he is used to that. He should be fine lying in his cage, perhaps with a towel over the top."

"An excellent suggestion, Shelbee. I'm so glad you could come. It's a relief having you care for Pablo." She glanced at me. "I'll let you go so you can talk with this young lady."

Shelbee nodded to me. "Sorry, forgot my manners. This is my friend, Clarissa Montgomery Hayes, and her dog, Paw. Clarissa let me introduce Patricia Carlson and Pablo."

I started to extend a hand to shake but realized that Pablo might not appreciate my reaching toward his owner. "Nice to meet you. It's Clarissa Brantford now."

I saw Shelbee's startled glance out of the corner of my eye.

I explained to Patricia. "Newlyweds." Fortunately, Shelbee didn't correct me.

Patricia smiled, saying, "Congratulations." She extended her hand giving mine a firm shake.

I was surprised as she appeared to be an anxious sort of person.

She must have sensed my surprise for she said, "I only get nervous at shows. Pablo means the world to me, and I don't want to do anything to upset him."

"I must admit to being nervous too. This is my first show, and I have no idea how it works or if Paw will cooperate. He can have a determined mindset. Determined to do things his way."

Shelbee's eyes widened further. She'd never known me to be interested in showing Paw or in his purebred status, but she covered her surprise well.

Patricia laughed. "Pablo is the same. And he usually gets his way, but he has become comfortable with the showing and always performs well. I'm sure you'll do fine. My advice would be to listen to Shelbee and trust your instincts. Avoid the owners who are competitive to a fault.

"How do you mean?"

She glanced around and lowered her voice. "Some competitions resulted in heated arguments, leading to fisticuffs. But that wasn't the worst. I've heard rumors that dogs were sabotaged."

Shelbee gasped. "That's terrible."

I instinctively pulled Paw closer to me. "How?"

Patricia held Pablo tighter to her. He looked up at her in concern.

"I'm not sure," she said, "but I heard of one dog being slipped a sedative, to make him too sleepy to compete.

The dog wasn't harmed seriously. I've never heard of any dog being hurt, just minor things to keep the dog from competing or performing his best."

I stroked Paw's neck comfortingly. "No wonder you are nervous."

Patricia eased her hold on Pablo. "Oh, don't worry, I shouldn't have probably said anything. I'm sure you will be fine. You are new and need more time competing before you would be serious competition to attract any kind of devious intent from other competitors. It's only at the higher levels that you need to worry."

Shelbee asked her, "But what about promising up and comers?"

"There were rumors about Phoenix King Horizon a few years ago. A beautiful Weimaraner who the rumors said was a perfect specimen of the breed. He'd started to win one show after the other. Then he disappeared from the shows. Rumor had it that he was no longer competitive, but no one knew why. Speculation had it that the dog was sabotaged at his last show. Something was put in his food. Some claimed that Connors was responsible."

Shelbee shook her head in disgust. "Sad. Competition is fine, but we should treat the dogs well. Keep Pablo close okay?"

Patricia nodded.

Shelbee motioned for me to follow her.

"Best of luck in the show," I called over my shoulder, as Paw and I followed Shelbee, who led me to a side room off the main hall.

It must have been planned as a small meeting room because a large conference table sat against one wall. The table held event brochures and complimentary candies and pens advertising the hotel. There were no windows. The walls and carpeting were the typical beige color found in many office settings. The chairs, used for the conference table, lined the walls. Two folding tables stood in the middle of the room, one laden with pastries and muffins. The second table contained a coffee urn and a tall dispenser labeled orange juice. Paper cups covered the rest of the table along with a stack of paper plates and plastic cutlery. Currently, the room was unoccupied.

Shelbee picked up a cup, filling it with orange juice. "This is where the complimentary meals are set out for the dog show fanciers. The judges get a more lavish setup in one of the side dining rooms. Now tell me what you are doing entering a dog show?"

"Don't you believe Paw is show material?"

"I think Paw will jump up on the judge and kiss his face then drag you across the hall at a gallop instead of obeying commands. He won't conform because you've spoilt him. You've always felt he was wonderful because he was himself, not because he was a purebred. Besides, he's not even registered so how can he enter a show. What gives?"

I laughed. "In a word, Bruce."

"You're on a case. I knew it!"

"Yes, but I'm coming to regret it. Bruce entered us in the show because he's tracking a suspect. He expects Paw and me to win his competitions so we can stay involved in the show. I'm nervous about this for all the reasons you mentioned. Paw is not show material."

"I agree he lacks discipline."

We both looked at Paw who had been slowly inching toward the pastry table. He suddenly flipped on his side giving us his best innocent look.

Shelbee just shook her head. "He is a purebred, though, and in my opinion, is in excellent form. Maybe a little heavy." She gave me a "significant" look. We had discussed how I spoiled Paw with too much food.

"Could he win in his breed?"

Shelbee finished her orange juice, throwing the cup in the trash. "He can on his form, but he has to behave too. He must tolerate the judge looking him over while he stands still. He needs to run across the ring, show good form, and stay in place, not bound around the ring. He can't get distracted in the ring and run over to the other dogs."

"In other words, we are sunk.".

My beloved dog inched closer to the pastries.

I loved him dearly, but I also knew his faults.

Shelbee watched Paw. "We can work with him. We have time before his breed is in the ring. There's a quiet park behind the hotel where we can practice. At least, it will give you a better chance in the ring."

$\mathcal{W}$e exited the room and walked through the hall into a side hallway. Owners were grooming their dogs as the hall bustled with activity, and others were rushing back and forth. I recognized Dorothy in her stall and saw Jed in another row talking to a man with a pug. The hotel staff was busy making last minute preparations before opening the hall to the show's spectators.

We walked down the side hallway which was blissfully quiet after all the activity in the hall. A subdued shade of blue carpet brightened the hallway while light sconces, placed at regular intervals along the beige walls, added warmth. Pleasant and serviceable but not meant to impress like the main areas of the hotel. The heavy side door exited onto a small park.

This one was smaller than the main dog park Paw and

I had visited on the other side of the hotel. Grass carpeted the small park and a few shrubs beside two picnic tables provided a little shade from the sun. The shrubs acted as a privacy screen.

Shelbee waved to encompass the area. "It's used by the hotel employees on break. Since everyone is involved in the show prep, we can practice here undisturbed for a while. The first thing we need to do is get Paw to accept being handled by the judge. He must stand still while the judge observes his stance, bone structure, and features, then accept the judge's hands on him. The judge will assess how Paw compares to the ideal for a Saint Bernard."

She shook her head. "I still can't believe Bruce got you into this show."

"I know. Bruce wanted to take Paw himself, but Paw refused to go without me. I don't know how he managed the paperwork or getting in at the last minute."

"I'm glad you came to the show. Paw will be calmer with you in the ring than he would with Bruce showing him."

Ruffling his hair, she said, "Now he has to listen and behave." She knelt, looking him in the eye as if she could convince him to do as she instructed.

He gave her his best "I am a good dog" look then slurped her face.

I crossed my arms, shaking my head. "That's what I am worried about."

She showed me how to stand properly. "Let's give it a try. I'll be the judge. You stand and hold his leash."

Paw sat down instead of standing, though.

I sighed.

Shelbee coaxed him to stand up and in the proper stance. "Now I look him over. He needs to stand still and look ahead."

So far, so good.

She stepped to his right to look at his form.

Paw turned his head to face her.

I tugged his leash. "No, Paw. Look forward."

Instead, he looked back at me.

Shelbee stepped in front of us. "I can see we have a lot of work to do."

I hung my head. "It's hopeless."

"Think positive." Shelbee went back to work with Paw. To my surprise, she got him to stand facing forward while she walked around him.

I guess I shouldn't have been surprised as I knew Shelbee was great with animals. She was a popular pet sitter and had a real rapport with pet clients.

Shelbee and Paw had advanced to the stage where the judge would physically examine him. It went well. Of course, Paw was familiar with Shelbee petting him. Would Paw tolerate a stranger?

Shelbee put her hands on her hips. "That's the best we can do right now. I would prefer to test him with someone he's not familiar with to see if he will obey. For now, let's move on to the running part.

"You will be required to fast walk, taking Paw up and back the ring to allow the judge to determine his gait and if it matches the breed's conformity."

She motioned us to do a trial run.

Paw and I ran back and forth. Being short, I always had a problem keeping up with Paw.

Shelbee coached us on how to set a good pace. Then she began to distract Paw. My job was to keep him focused and moving. After several attempts, we seemed to get the hang of it.

Until the side door to the park opened and Bruce stepped out.

Paw turned at the sound, pulled the leash from my grip, and ran to Bruce.

I groaned.

Paw jumped up and lunged at Bruce who braced for the impact, aware of Paw's antics.

Paw slurped Bruce's face.

All three of us spoke in unison, "No! Get down Paw."

Paw got down but gave us his sad puppy look.

Shelbee and I walked over to Bruce who brushed his clothes off.

Shelbee crossed her arms. "That didn't work."

Bruce raised an eyebrow. "What didn't work?"

"Paw was supposed to stay with Clarissa and finish his run through for the judge, not run over to you."

Bruce looked around the empty park. "What judge?"

I picked up Paw's leash. "She means herself. We're

practicing and trying to train Paw to behave in the ring for his judging. Shelbee has been a big help to me, but Paw refuses to cooperate."

Bruce scratched Paw's ears. "Doesn't Paw know how to work in the judging ring? I mean it can't be that hard just to stand there and then run a little."

Shelbee rolled her eyes as I shook my head, thinking he was an idiot.

He must have read our thoughts. "I'm an idiot, right?"

Shelbee rolled her eyes. "Way to go, Mr. Private Detective."

Her tone indicated that she was becoming frustrated by her inability to get Paw to behave.

I understood her feelings but knew how Paw could be.

She gestured for us to follow her over to where we had been practicing. "Since you are here, you might as well help us."

As we followed Shelbee, I asked Bruce, "Did you find out anything when you followed Matt Monroe?"

He hesitated and looked toward Shelbee.

I grinned. "She knows."

Bruce gave me a frustrated look.

Today, Paw and I had that effect on people.

I shrugged. "I had to tell her something. She knows I'd never enter a dog show on my own. I figured the truth was best. Besides, Shelbee has been a big help in my other investigations."

"Yes, I have."

Bruce nodded his agreement. "I followed Monroe to the lobby where he made a phone call. I couldn't get close enough to hear his call, but by his hand gestures, he seemed agitated. Then he went up to the hotel room across from ours. I assume it's his room."

Shelbee asked, "Why would you be following Matt?"

Bruce and I chorused, "You know him?"

"I've talked to him at some of the dog shows. He seemed like a nice guy, always helping his aunt who is a client of mine."

I blinked. "I didn't know you went to dog shows."

"I've gone to a few. It comes with acting as a pet sitter as some of my clients are on the dog show circuit. Often they want someone to come along and help keep their dog calm at a show since shows can be exhausting even for the most avid dogs."

Bruce and I exchanged a glance then faced Shelbee, who raised her hands. "What?"

I tilted my head toward Shelbee, "Ask her."

"Shelbee, would you help us with this investigation?"

"Why I thought you'd never ask, Bruce? Of course, I'll help, but we need to get Paw ready for his big debut."

"How can I help?"

"You can be the judge."

The three of us attempted to train Paw for the judging ring. He tolerated Bruce examining him and running his hands over his body as a judge would do.

I practiced running back and forth with Paw. He did well with a few corrections from Shelbee. I doubted this would work in the ring with a stranger, but it was a good start.

We finished and sat down at the picnic table to discuss the case. Paw lolled in the shade of the shrubs.

I sat across from Bruce, adjusting to the hard bench seat. "Did you get to question the guy from the park?"

Shelbee tapped my hand. "What guy?"

"There was a tall guy in the park with a mastiff, discussing Lyon's death with a woman who had a Maltese. Neither indicated they thought Lyon's death was murder, but from the conversation, the guy hated Lyon."

Bruce clasped his hands on the picnic table. "No. I couldn't find him in the crowded hall. I asked the security staff about him, but with no name and all the activity going on, they were no help. I'm certain he's the guy I suspect. I'll keep looking, and I'll watch for him at the mastiff judging. That's the quickest way to find him."

Shelbee asked, "What's the name of the guy you suspect?"

"Gerald Hoffman."

"Tall guy, surly disposition?"

"Yes, do you know him?"

"I know of him, and I've seen him at the shows but never talked to him. Don't want to. He has a nasty temper and isn't friendly. Most of the dog owners are kind and pleasant people. Not this guy. I must admit he treats his dog well. But don't get in the way or disparage his dog. He'll take off your head. I've seen him snarl at a spectator who thought his dog was a little heavy. Most of the other owners give him a wide berth."

I shuddered. "Hoffman sounds awful."

Bruce leaned forward. "I discovered Hoffman had a fight with Connors at a previous show."

Shelbee glanced at me. "Connors? Lyon Connors?"

"Yes. I forgot to tell you whose death Bruce was investigating."

"Lyon Connors is dead? Well, that will make a lot of people happy."

Bruce and I gaped at her.

"Lyon Connors was hated by most of the fanciers. He had a few friends, but many more enemies. He was a fierce competitor. One of the worst. There were rumors that he did underhanded things like drugging competing dogs to prevent them from performing in the ring. He wasn't above going after the owners and the newbies either."

I glanced at Paw. "What do you mean, newbies?"

"Most of the fierce competition happens at the upper levels where the top dogs have gotten the most points. Even there, most contestants respect each other. There are some who can go too far to win any way they can. But the unspoken rule is to leave the new entrants alone until they build to the higher level. Many of them won't make it to the upper levels so that they won't be a problem. Besides, even the fierce competitors have respect for anyone willing to try showing. Connors didn't care if you were a newbie or not. He would try to knock out anyone he considered the competition. I don't know how Dorothy and her husband could be friends with him. Hoffman certainly wasn't."

Bruce asked, "How much did they hate each other?"

I said, "Is that what Patricia was talking about?" I explained to Bruce, "Patricia is one of Shelbee's clients and is here for the competition. She told us about incidences at previous shows where, according to rumor, sabotage caused show losses."

Shelbee shook her head. "Patricia worries too much. Hoffman and Connors did get into a heated argument that came to blows. I didn't see it, but Patricia told me about it. As I understand it, Connors accused Hoffman of feeding a drug-laced treat to his dog. Security had to pull them apart. I don't know if Hoffman did anything or if Connors had become paranoid. By the way, what happened to Lucille Duvee Carns the third?"

We asked, "Who?"

"Lucille is Connors's dog. Is she all right?"

Bruce nodded. "Connors's sister has the dog and plans to keep her. As far as I know, she's not going to show Lucille. Margaret, that's Connors's sister, thinks the dog shows were silly."

"That is a sentiment that would be unpopular with this crowd," said Shelbee. "I am glad Lucille will be loved.

She is a sweet dog. I know there will be a lot of relieved dog owners who won't have to compete against her."

"Connors's dog was at the upper level?"

"Yes. Lucille was one of the best, if not the best, Chihuahua."

I drummed the table with my fingers. "Other Chihuahua owners may have had a grudge against Lucille and Connors. Enough to kill for?"

Shelbee asked, "Is that what you are thinking? That one of the dog show owners would kill? I can't see it. There's a big jump from sabotage to murder."

"But not entirely implausible," said Bruce. "Especially if you wanted your dog to win and another dog stood in the way."

I stopped drumming my fingers. "You are thinking of Matt Monroe."

He nodded.

Shelbee shrugged. "I hope not. Besides, Matt doesn't do the shows usually. His aunt is the dog enthusiast. If not for her broken hip, she would be here. Her dog was strong competition to Lucille." She raised her hand when I began to speak. "It wouldn't have to be another Chihuahua owner. Lucille ended up in the Best in Show category frequently, making other breed owners just as much a suspect as Matt."

"That's a lot of suspects." Bruce shook his head. "I need to find a way to narrow them down. I wish I knew more about Connors, but his sister knew little about his dog show involvement."

I turned to Shelbee. "Didn't you say Dorothy and her husband were friends with Connors? I met a Dorothy last evening. She had a Pomeranian in her arms. I didn't meet her husband, though. Is she the Dorothy you mean?"

"That's her. Dorothy Hawkins. You didn't meet her husband, Fred, because he died last year. He lost control of his car on an icy road and crashed. Killed instantly. I heard that Dorothy was distraught, but she decided to keep showing because it was Fred's passion. Hers too, if you ask me. She could tell you all about Connors."

"Great! I can speak to her right now. Maybe we can learn something important."

Shelbee was shaking her head as I spoke. "No way. First of all, you are due in the ring in a half hour and need to get dressed. Second, Dorothy will be engrossed in the show. She won't spare a minute to talk with you. The show always comes first."

I looked down at my freshly pressed jeans and knit shirt. "Get dressed? I am dressed."

"No, you are not. You must dress up for the judging ring. Please tell me you brought a skirt and nice blouse?"

Shocked, my mouth dropped open.

Shelbee shook her head. "Just go up to your room. I'll get you some dressier clothes from the hotel gift shop. I'd lend you mine, but they would never fit."

Bruce covered his mouth with his hand, no doubt to hide a smile. "Good luck. I'm going to hang around the hall and see who I can talk to."

I glared at him.

Shelbee nudged me toward the entrance to the hotel. "Go on up. I'll bring the clothes and groom Paw for the ring while you dress."

Paw and I went.

CHAPTER 4

I rushed through my shower then dressed in the clothes Shelbee had brought me – a black skirt and a light blue blouse.

Paw's coat gleamed from his grooming session.

Shelbee stepped back and examined us. "You look presentable. Paw's appearance will have to do."

I looked down at my dear Saint Bernard.

Have to do? Paw's coat gleamed, in the best groomed conditioned I had ever seen it.

Shelbee placed my numbered band around my upper arm. She, Paw, and I walked down to the hall to the elevator. We rode to the foyer, walked to the hall, and proceeded to the Saint Bernard judging ring.

The ring, set up in a circular arena, sectioned off part of the larger hall used for conventions at the hotel. Right above us, the fluorescent lights cast a hard, cold light down on everyone. The area was roped off to keep the spectators out of the ring so they wouldn't interfere with the judging. A wooden platform, placed near the middle of the ring, would be used for the dog to stand on while the judges did their examination and review.

Three other entrants were lined up in a row behind the platform.

Shelbee stopped at the edge of the ring. She slipped something into my pocket. "I'll wait for you here. Remember to keep Paw on your left side. Don't worry. You'll do great."

As we were talking, a ring attendant was motioning to me to get in line. I turned to the ring, but a large man bumped into my back.

"My apologies," he said with a crisp, British accent. As he hurried past me, I saw a beautiful Saint Bernard trotting at his side. Man and dog took their place in the judging line-up.

I waved to Shelbee, who mouthed "Good luck," as I hurried to get in line too.

Crossing to the line-up, I surveyed my competition. All four of the Saint Bernards looked to be perfect specimens of their breed. The owners were a mixed lot, but all appeared poised and confident.

The first entrant was called up to the platform. Her Saint Bernard, displaying the beautiful big brown eyes of the breed and a luxurious coat, stood like a statue, perfectly behaved.

The woman was perfectly groomed as well and wore

a plum-colored suit with a white blouse. Sensible, low heeled shoes completed her ensemble.

The judge, a petite woman of middle age with a few streaks of gray in her hair, began her review by studying the dog's face. She moved to each side and around behind him, as Shelbee had demonstrated, then the judge ran her hands over the dog's head, shoulders, and back. She examined his tail, I assumed for fullness, and returned to stare at his face.

The Saint Bernard stood still for this examination.

The judge motioned for the dog's owner to take him up and back at a quick run. The pair moved in perfect unison. The dog didn't drag the woman or vary from his task. All she did was tug on the leash, and he responded. I noticed she offered him a whiff of a dog treat to perform and when finished gave him the treat.

Now I realized what Shelbee had slipped in my pocket and why. The treat was to get Paw's attention and good behavior. I hoped it worked.

The first entrant returned to the line-up, and the next one went up to the platform. They continued in this way through the next entrant and then the guy next to me.

Paw shifted, restless to move, so I caressed his head, calming him for the moment.

The British guy, who had bumped into me, was on the platform. He was a handsome man in a gray suit and a white shirt and striped tie. Even the judge seemed to blush when he smiled at her. I guessed his age at late twenties, maybe thirty.

His dog, as beautiful a specimen as his owner, had long, luxurious white and brown fur with soulful brown eyes on a solid Saint Bernard frame.

The judge showed no other emotion, but I was impressed.

The pair went through the routine as instructed and returned to stand next to me.

Now it was our turn.

I whispered to Paw, "Please behave and do this for us."

The British guy gave me a reassuring smile, even though we were competing against him.

Paw and I stepped up to the platform.

I felt underdressed in my skirt and blouse. My palms felt slick, and a bead of sweat ran down my back. Taking a deep breath, I held Paw as still as I could.

The judge gave me a gentle smile and proceeded to study Paw. As she stepped to each side and behind, I hoped that Paw stayed looking ahead.

I sighed with relief when he obeyed but knew we had two more hurdles to jump before I could relax.

The judge came around front and began to touch Paw's head and frame.

He moved a fraction, and I gave an infinitesimal tug on the leash to stop his movement.

He settled, and the judge completed her examination. She nodded to me to walk him.

I took the treat out of my pocket, gave him a sniff, and moved him off the platform to start our walk.

Here was my real challenge. Would Paw stay in line or run off to the side? Could I control him and keep up?

We ran down the length of the ring, and I kept up. We turned, and I sensed his eagerness to run straight back to the judge at a gallop.

I tugged on the leash, reining him in enough to keep him in line.

He trotted back almost too fast for me to keep up, but I held onto him and didn't fall. I appreciated the wisdom of wearing sensible shoes.

The judge smiled and motioned us back to the platform. I was a little confused since no one else had had to go back to the platform. She took a final look at Paw and motioned us back in line.

I slipped Paw his treat.

By their expressions, it seemed the other entrants were surprised at Paw's second examination. They all looked at us with more curiosity than when we first entered. I had got the impression that we had been dismissed as no threat when we first had entered. Now we were being reappraised.

The judge went to her assistant and consulted her notebook then returned to us. She motioned the British guy out in a new line-up with Paw and I next followed by the plum-suited woman and the next two entrants.

I was surprised since I thought the British guy's Saint Bernard was the best. And it turned out I was right for the judge named him number one, Paw and I number two and on down the line.

My mouth dropped open.

The plum-suited woman grimaced in disgust and stalked off.

The judge came over and shook my hand. "He's beautiful. With a little more work, you will soon be in the top spot." She turned to talk to the British guy.

I gasped – second place, and a compliment from the judge. We hurried over to Shelbee, Paw's tail waving in triumph.

"I knew you could do it," she said as we both gave Paw a big hug.

The British guy walked up, extending his hand. "Great work! Allow me to introduce myself. Colin Sikes."

Paw sniffed at his dog who sniffed back. They seemed to like each other.

I took his hand. "Clarissa Hay...Brantford." I gestured to Shelbee, saying, "This is my friend, Shelbee."

He lifted my hand and kissed it then did the same to Shelbee's. "A pleasure to meet such lovely ladies." He motioned to his Saint Bernard. "Allow me to introduce another lovely lady. This is Petula Delicious Snifflewood. Pettie, for short."

I smiled. "A pleasure to meet you, my lady. May I introduce my gentleman friend - Paw."

Colin laughed. "He's a fine-looking fellow. I wanted to apologize again for bumping into you. It gets hectic on show days."

"No problem."

"I can see I will have competition from you in the future. I look forward to seeing you again."

He gave me a dazzling smile and walked off.

I blushed as Shelbee sighed.

A familiar voice behind me huffed, "Who was that?"

I hadn't heard Bruce walk up behind me. "His name is Colin Sikes. He won the Saint Bernard competition."

"Humph." Bruce asked Shelbee, "You know him?"

"Not really. I've heard of the guy. He is a British ex-pat and considered an excellent breeder. His Saint Bernards are frequent winners and have placed well in Best of Show in the past. It doesn't hurt that he is really cute." She giggled.

I grinned at Bruce's sour expression.

He said, "I'll check him out."

Shelbee winked at me and then said to Bruce, "I think he's too handsome to be a suspect, don't you, 'Rissa?"

"Definitely."

Bruce just glared at Shelbee and put his arm around me. He was rather possessive, but I knew he meant well. If it had been a beautiful woman smiling at Bruce, I would be a little possessive too.

I leaned my head on his shoulder. "Well now that I am out of any further competition, what do we do next?"

Bruce pulled me closer to avoid being bumped by people hurrying around us. "We need to talk to Hoffman, Dorothy, and any other competitors who may have bene-fited from Connors's death."

Shelbee's smile vanished. "What if his death isn't connected to the dog show?"

"We have to start somewhere, and the dog show is happening now. That gives us our best lead."

I scratched Paw's ears as he shifted his weight from paw to paw. He hated standing in one place too long. "It sounds to me like showing his dog was Connors's main passion. Perhaps if it is personal, it involves someone here at the show. These are the people he interacted with a good bit of the time."

Bruce nodded. "That's true. I checked out his family, but other than his sister he avoided them. His will left everything to his sister to care for his dog, and I have thoroughly checked out the sister. Connors was retired and had no friends outside the show world."

"Let's concentrate on the show people, asking around about Connors. Maybe we can uncover something about Connors's relationships with other entrants."

Paw whined, straining at his leash as people hustled past us.

"It's best to wait to talk to Dorothy," said Shelbee, "but you can go watch the mastiff ring and talk with Hoffman after the competition ends. I'll take Paw to the attached park so he can relax after his performance."

I handed her Paw's leash, knelt, and hugged Paw. "You did great, big fella!"

He wagged his tail enthusiastically.

I released him, and they walked off.

Spectators crowded the arena, forcing us to weave around people to get to the mastiff judging ring. We arrived in time to see the judging start. Seven dogs competed in this ring, each one in perfect form. Of course, judging could come down to the merest details that I would never fully grasp.

Gerald Hoffman was the fourth in line. Even now he wore a slight scowl. His mastiff stood at rigid attention.

The first owner walked her dog for the judge. Her mastiff obediently stayed with her, moderating his pace to her shorter one.

I was surprised to see how well she handled him since she appeared elderly, but she put on a masterful show.

The judge, a man who looked to be in his mid-thirties, nodded in satisfaction when they returned to him. He spoke a few words to the elderly lady, and she returned to the line-up.

The judging continued with the next two contestants.

A young Hispanic man wearing a red shirt and black pants maneuvered his mastiff with finesse through his judging. Both man and dog moved in step as if dancing.

The judge smiled as they took their walk then nodded them to step back in line.

The third entrant, a young woman about my age, wore a green pantsuit which complemented her long, curly, red hair. Her mastiff appeared to be the perfect representative of the breed.

The judge took longer examining this dog. He nodded indicating for the red-haired girl to walk her mastiff.

The dog stood solid and strong with perfect coloring for his breed. The red-haired girl and her mastiff would be tough to beat.

Then disaster happened.

A white terrier came bolting into the ring.

All the mastiffs lifted their heads, on alert and ready to give chase.

The red-haired woman's mastiff lunged toward the terrier who was running around him, barking frantically. The young woman tried desperately to hold onto her dog's leash and control him. He lunged again and pulled the leash from her hands.

Both dogs ran out of the ring, but the judge acted quickly and called in help. The PA system announced that dogs were loose and required all owners secure their dogs.

The red-haired woman ran from the ring after her dog as the judge motioned to the other mastiff owners to stay in place. What could have been a disaster was soon under control thanks to the show volunteers' quick action. Within minutes the PA announced that the capture of the loose dogs and word spread that no harm had come to dog or person.

The red-haired girl returned to the ring with her mastiff, head hanging in defeat. Several of the other mastiff owners nodded in commiseration, aware that it could happen to any of them. Several of them had had to struggle to hold their dogs. What irritated me was the smug expression on Gerald Hoffman's face. He had no sympathy for his fellow competitor.

The judge offered the woman a second chance to walk her dog. This time things went better, but the mastiff was nervous and jumpy. The judge nodded, and they returned to the lineup.

Now it was Hoffman's turn. He and his mastiff strode up to the judge. The mastiff stood still staring straight ahead as the judge performed his examination. He ran his hands over the mastiff's broad head continuing over his back. The mastiff's beautifully sleek, tan coat glowed under the ring lights displaying a well-defined muscula-ture. Satisfied, the judge nodded to Hoffman to walk his dog. This time no interruptions occurred and man and dog performed the walk to perfection. They returned to the judge, who with one final exam, sent them back to the line of contestants.

As Hoffman turned, I saw a smirk on his face.

The last three contestants went through their judging. Each performed well, but they lacked the perfection of Hoffman's mastiff or the grace that the first contestant and her dog had shown. Once the judging was complete, the judge spent several minutes deliberating and recording information in his notebook. Once he completed his notes, he returned to the entrants and began pulling out his choices, gesturing to a new line up.

The first contestant, the elderly lady, was first in line. Hoffman was next, then the young Hispanic man, followed by contestants six, five, seven, and sadly, the third contestant, the young woman whose dog had misbehaved.

The elderly lady won the competition.

The judge smiled at the elderly lady. "Ladies and gentleman, I present the winners of the mastiff breed competition – Ina Holmes and her mastiff, Max."

The spectators applauded.

Hoffman's smug expression turned to a deep scowl. He ignored the other owners, who congratulated the winner and consoled the young woman.

The young Hispanic man and the elderly lady accompanied the young woman from the ring.

Contestants five, six, and seven followed with their heads together, gesturing and talking with smiles on their faces.

Not so in the ring. Gerald Hoffman had approached the judge. Their conversation was indistinct at first as they were too far away for me to hear. But that quickly changed as Hoffman's voice rose along with his temper.

CHAPTER 5

*B*y now, everyone in the vicinity was watching the confrontation.

Hoffman's voice rose as he berated the judge's decision. "What kind of judge are you? Are you even qualified to be in the ring?"

"Mr. Hoffman I can assure you I am qualified. I have been judging for several years now, and I stand by my decision of this competition. You have a beautiful mastiff, but he wasn't the best dog on this day. It happens."

"It doesn't happen to me. You are judging foolishly using sentimentality over an old woman and her dog that doesn't have the pedigree that mine does."

"As I said, I stand by my decision, and since I'm the judge, my ruling is final."

"Not for long, if I have anything to say about it. I'm reporting you."

Hoffman stormed out of the ring with his mastiff

trotting beside him. The dog had remained quiet throughout the confrontation.

Hoffman breezed past us. Several of the other show judges went over to the mastiff judge, commiserating with him.

Bruce watched Hoffman stride away. "I'm going to follow him and question him once he calms down."

I nodded in agreement. "I'll question some of the other mastiff owners about Hoffman."

"Good idea." Bruce gave me a half-smile and turned to follow Hoffman.

I didn't know where the mastiff breeders were set up in the hall. I headed in the direction of the closest entrant stalls to ask directions to the mastiffs. The third owner I spoke to was able to direct me to the mastiff area. I walked through rows of Labrador retrievers and Irish setters where the dogs' owners groomed them for the ring. Their luxurious coats shone brightly and brought a smile to my face. Some of the dogs stood calmly, enjoying the grooming attention while others fidgeted, eager to be active and moving.

I turned at the end of the row and entered the greyhound area where poised and sleek dogs lay curled in their beds or cages. Several lay placidly beside their owners. The greyhounds retained a grace I marveled at seeing. The breed had finished their judging earlier in the day, and cages proudly displayed winning ribbons. A few show attendants walked the aisles observing the dogs and discussing their merits.

I left the greyhounds behind. Stepping into the next aisle, I found the mastiffs. Big, solid dogs stared at me through soulful brown eyes. The older lady, Ina Holmes, who had won the competition was conversing with the young woman whose dog had performed badly. The young Hispanic man stood in his stall next to them. All three mastiffs were settled contentedly at the feet of their owners.

I approached their group with a smile on my face and extended my hand to Ina Holmes. "Hello. I don't mean to intrude, but I wanted to congratulate you on your win."

"Thank you." She smiled.

"You have a beautiful mastiff, and I was impressed with how well you handled him."

She stiffened, her smile fading, and spoke with a sharp tone. "I know how to communicate with my dog. Being older doesn't mean I am feeble."

"I wasn't implying that it did."

"Sorry." She relaxed her muscles. "A lot of people assume I can't handle my dog just because I am older than them. It gets extremely insulting and frustrating."

The young woman said, "Ina is the best dog handler I know," as the Hispanic man nodded in agreement.

I raised a hand in placation. "I'm sure she is. I meant no disrespect, if anything, I was referring to your small stature like mine. I have a Saint Bernard who I have trouble controlling because he is so large. You handled your Mastiff so gracefully that I was envious."

Ina's smile returned. "I had trouble controlling Max

here at first too. He always would outdistance me. The more you work with your dog, the more in tune you will become, and he will be willing to moderate his pace to you."

The young woman moaned, "That is if he doesn't go chasing off after other dogs."

"That was unfortunate," Ina consoled her, "but it could have happened to any of us. The ring is supposed to be free from that kind of incident. Don't beat yourself up over bad luck."

She turned back to me, saying, "We forgot to introduce ourselves. I'm Ina Holmes. This young lady is Rachel Foster, and this young man is Alex Cortez."

She pointed to the dogs. "This is Max. Rachel owns Caleb and Alex owns Manny."

"Short for Manuel." The young man smiled fondly at his dog.

I remembered my fake name. "I'm Clarissa Brantford. Paw, my Saint Bernard, is with my friend, Shelbee."

Ina asked, "Shelbee Van Vight?"

"Yes, do you know her?"

"Yes, I do. She is the best dog sitter I have ever encountered."

"I agree. She helped me prepare for this show since it is the first time I have been in one. I was nervous that something would go wrong. I was wondering, how often does what happened to Rachel occur in the ring?"

"It's rare," Ina replied. "There are volunteers around the ring who are trained to respond quickly to such interruptions and prevent any other dogs or people from entering the ring."

Alex huffed. "Sabotage, if you ask me."

"Alex! That is unprofessional. You should be careful voicing that opinion. Dogs do get away from their owners at times."

"Ina, you know as well as I do that some owners will do anything to win. Gerald Hoffman is one of them. You can bet he was hoping to benefit from the dog running into the ring whether he caused it or not. He sure was angry about losing."

Rachel grinned at Ina. "I bet Hoffman never thought you would win. I'm furious that he believes you only won because the judge was sympathetic to you. He can be a real jerk."

"I'll admit he can be a challenge," said Ina.

I leaned forward. "Alex, you said that Hoffman might have been responsible for the loose dog. Has he done something like that in the past?"

"Not like this incident. But I've heard rumors accusing Hoffman of ruining other owners' chances in the ring."

Ina scratched her dog's back. "Alex may be referring to when Chancy Collins fell last year. Gerald was standing next to him during registration, and his dog's leash accidentally tripped Chancy. Poor Chance had to miss the competition from a badly twisted ankle."

"That's not all, Ina, and you know it. Hoffman isn't the only one who pulls these kinds of things. Lyon Connors benefitted several times from another owner's misfortunes."

I asked, "Did Connors cause those misfortunes?"

"No one could prove anything, but yes, I think he did." Alex could see Ina was about to protest, so he continued. "And I'm not the only one who thinks it."

"Did Connors try something on Hoffman?"

Rachel and Alex looked to Ina to answer.

Sighing, she said, "Those two never got along. Connors made a lot of enemies. I am sorry he's dead, but by the time he died, he had few friends besides Dorothy. I guess she felt kind to him since he and her husband had been friends, but I can't think of anyone else who still liked him. He and Hoffman had had numerous arguments at shows over the years."

Alex asked Ina, "Didn't Connors accuse Hoffman of trying to drug his dog last year at the Belfont show?"

"Yes, he did. They came to blows over it. Both were in the Best in Show category. Connors swore Hoffman had tried to slip a drug-laced treat to his dog. The treat, if it existed, disappeared before the show officials could sort everything out. Connors took out an official complaint against Hoffman and tried to get him blacklisted from competition, but without any proof, the officials couldn't do anything."

Could this be the motive for Connors's death?

"Do you think Hoffman was trying to drug the dog?"

Alex replied, "Most likely. Of course, it didn't do him any good. Dorothy's husband won the competition. I always wondered if it hadn't been Fred who had the drugged treat. He and Dorothy were right there when the incident occurred, and they both took competing to an extreme."

"Do you mean Dorothy Hawkins? I met her yesterday. Is Dorothy's husband at the show?"

Ina answered. "Yes, that is Dorothy, but her husband isn't here. Sadly, Fred died in a car accident about six months ago. I thought she wouldn't come to this show, but she said she is doing it in her husband's memory."

Shelbee arrived with Paw who was as happy to greet the other dogs as Shelbee was. A lot of sniffing and mild woofing ensued amongst the dogs.

Ina gestured to Alex and Rachel and their dogs. "Shelbee, let me introduce Alex Cortez and Rachel Foster. Alex owns Manny and Rachel owns Caleb."

Shelbee extended her hand to Alex and then Rachel. "Nice to meet you."

We talked with the three mastiff owners a few minutes then left to return to Paw's stall.

As we walked through the aisles, Shelbee asked, "Any luck finding out about Hoffman?"

"I learned some information and gossip, but I don't know if it is relevant."

I recapped everything Ina, Alex, and Rachel told me.

Shelbee said, "Interesting. I wonder..." but stopped

and looked further up the aisle at the sound of two men arguing.

One was Matt Monroe who was holding one of his aunt's Chihuahuas protectively against his chest.

The other was Hoffman whose face was red and whose voice kept getting louder. "You little shrimp. Get out of my way!"

Matt stood his ground.

Hoffman's mastiff looked tense and alert which concerned me. I would not have put it past Hoffman to command the dog to attack. The mastiff seemed to be eyeing the Chihuahua as a snack.

Paw must have thought so, too, because he pulled from Shelbee's grasp and trotted to the two arguing men. He stepped between them, acting as a shield for Matt and his Chihuahua. Paw didn't assume an aggressive stance. Instead, he stood with his head up, alert for trouble from the mastiff.

Hoffman looked down at Paw. "What is this?" he demanded. "Now you got a bodyguard?"

Pointing at Paw, he said, "Get out of here!"

Paw stood firm.

Ignoring Hoffman's outburst, I ran to Paw, afraid that Hoffman would hurt him.

I stopped as I saw Bruce approach from the opposite direction.

Bruce inserted himself between Hoffman and Matt, facing Hoffman with his laser stare. "That's enough arguing for now. You are disturbing the other owners and dogs, plus your dog is too tense. Go cool down."

Hoffman grunted, "This is none of your business," as he stepped closer to Bruce, crowding him.

Paw gave a low growl.

The mastiff responded with a growl of its own.

Hoffman stopped and glanced down at his dog. He returned a glare to Bruce, gave a quick command to his dog, and stalked off.

I sighed in relief after Hoffman passed Shelbee and me in the aisle. I glanced around and saw that several other people were breathing easier.

Bruce bent and retrieved Paw's leash then turned to Matt. "You all right?"

"I could have handled him. He's just a bully."

Bruce nodded but didn't say anything.

When Shelbee and I reached Bruce's side, I took Paw's leash from him. "What was that all about?"

Matt cuddled Lila. "I told Hoffman he should leave Ken Topelo alone."

I had no idea who Ken Topelo was, and it must have shown on my face for Matt continued. "He is the one who was judging the mastiffs. Hoffman had no cause to lodge a complaint against him."

A young woman walked up to us. She smiled at every-one, took Matt's hand, and asked him, "You all right?"

He smiled at her and then introduced her. "This is Colby Gerard, a friend of mine."

Shelbee and I smiled. "Hello."

Bruce nodded.

Matt handed Lila to Colby. "If you will excuse us, we need to get Lila back to her stall." They walked away, Matt wrapping an arm around Colby's shoulders.

I realized we were standing in the Chihuahua section where several owners stood in their stalls cuddling adorable tan Chihuahuas. A few dogs were eating out of bowls nearly as big as they were in size.

My stomach grumbled. "Let's get lunch somewhere."

Bruce patted his stomach. "I could eat."

Shelbee laughed. "Why doesn't that surprise me? I heard the hotel's café serves good food."

I hesitated. "What about Paw?"

Shelbee hugged me. "No worries, dogs are welcome at this cafe."

We left the hall, cutting diagonally across the hotel's main reception area to a charming little cafe on the other side. It resembled a French-style open air café with a red and white striped awning jutting out from the front of it. Under the awning were placed three sets of tables and chairs. Behind these were glass windows with a glass door between them. The door was propped open, and delicious smells wafted out. Through the windows could be seen more tables and chairs in intimate groupings. A long counter ran along the back wall where various pastries and desserts were displayed.

The lunch hour was just beginning so only a few people occupied tables inside. A waitress was pouring coffee for a couple at one of them.

We chose to sit outside so that Paw had more room to stretch out. We took the end table to the left of the cafe so Paw wouldn't trip anyone. The right-side table had a young woman and her Pomeranian who sat on a chair next to her. She wore black sweatpants and a bright pink T-shirt. The T-shirt's color matched the bow in her dog's hair. The center table was unoccupied.

The waitress soon appeared with menus, and we placed our drinks order. I chose water with lemon while Shelbee requested herbal tea and Bruce wanted coffee.

I set my menu aside. "Can I have a bowl of water to give my dog?"

"Sure."

We spent several minutes perusing the menu.

Bruce and I each chose a cheeseburger and fries.

Shelbee looked at us in disappointment. She had become health conscious choosing to eat more wholesome foods.

The waitress returned with our drinks and water for Paw, which I set down to him.

He began drinking while the waitress took our orders.

Shelbee chose a large salad with strips of chicken breast and vinaigrette dressing.

I teased her, "Bunny food."

"You need to eat healthier, Ms. Cheeseburger."

"Hey, I need the protein to keep my strength up. Paw is a strong dog. It takes a lot to hold onto his leash."

"You're not going to be able to keep up with him if you keep eating junk food."

Bruce drank some coffee then said, "Cheeseburgers aren't junk food. They're a gift from the gods."

Paw woofed.

The young woman and her Pomeranian glanced at us, eyebrow raised.

I smiled and waved to her.

She responded with a faint smile and returned to her lunch.

I took a sip of my water. "My guess is you weren't able to talk to Hoffman before the confrontation he had with Matt?"

Bruce raised his eyebrow. "What makes you say that?"

"It didn't look like Hoffman knew you when you stepped in the middle of that argument."

"No, he didn't. I was about to talk to him when he got into that fight. Probably ruined my chances of approaching him on casual terms. He'll be on guard and unwilling to talk now."

Shelbee took a sip of her tea. "Is the guy ever in a good mood?"

The waitress arrived with our food, setting our plates down and handing me a blue plate. "For your furry friend."

"Thank you."

Shelbee nodded to the blue plate. "I didn't know the cafe would supply dog dishes."

"It was planned for this weekend while the dog show is here. People love the dishes, and the owner is considering doing it full time. Most of the customers are fine with it except for a few who are worried they could be eating off a plate a dog licked. I explain that the blue ones are for the dogs and assure them that we wash them separately."

She returned to a customer inside the cafe.

I placed a piece of burger on the plate and set it down for Paw, who quickly devoured it.

I warned Shelbee, "Don't say a word to the vet."

Paw's vet was constantly reminding me not to feed Paw people food. Of course, I would never feed him something dangerous like chocolate, but a little burger seemed fine for a treat.

I turned to Bruce. "What next?"

He picked up his cheeseburger. "I'm going to track down Hoffman after lunch and attempt to question him. If necessary, I'll tell him that I'm a private detective. I will get my questions answered."

"Let me talk to him. He may respond better to me."

"No way. That guy is too volatile. I don't want you near him."

"It's not like we'll be alone. I'll talk to Hoffman in the hall where plenty of people are near me. I'll be perfectly fine. I can take care of myself, Bruce."

Shelbee pushed her salad away. "I'll go with you."

I shook my head. "No. I need you to watch Paw."

He looked up at me when I said his name.

I reached down and patted his head. "I don't want him near Hoffman's mastiff. A dog fight is the last thing we need. If Hoffman gets angry, I know Paw will go into defense mode which would set the mastiff to doing the same."

Shelbee grumbled. "I want to help with the investigation too."

"Why don't you talk with Matt's girlfriend, Colby Gerard? Maybe you can find out what Matt and Hoffman were arguing about."

"You think it wasn't about Ken Topelo?"

"No. I don't."

Bruce relented. "All right. You try to talk to Hoffman. I'm not happy about it, but you may have more luck than me. While Shelbee talks with Ms. Gerard, I'm going to talk to Matt Monroe."

A voice at my shoulder, said, "Did you mention Colby Gerard?" The young woman with the Pomeranian stood next to our table with her dog in her arms.

We had been so busy talking I hadn't seen her walk over to us.

I nodded. "Yes, do you know Colby?"

"I used to. I haven't seen her in over a year. Do you happen to know how I can contact her?"

Bruce stood up. "You are?"

"Carolyn Devoe. Colby used to care for Roscoe here." She indicated the Pomeranian.

I started to say, "She is here at the show," but Bruce interrupted.

"Used to?"

Carolyn's eyes widened. "She's here. You've seen her?"

I nodded.

Responding to Bruce, she said, "Colby was the best pet sitter I ever had. One of the dog owners accused her of negligence, and she dropped out of sight."

Bruce asked, "Who was the owner?"

I held my breath. Could it have been Hoffman?

Carolyn fidgeted with her Pomeranian's leash that she had gripped in her hand. "Well ... I hate to speak ill of another owner, let alone a dead one but it was Lyon Connors."

I stood up. "It sounds as though Connors didn't get along with anyone."

"Not many that I know of."

Paw had stood up and was trying to sniff Roscoe who gave a yip in greeting.

Carolyn cuddled Roscoe. "I better go. I'll see if I can find Colby in the hall. If you speak with her, could you tell her I want to see her?"

We nodded, and she hurried off with Roscoe in her arms.

Paw lay back down with a sigh. He loved to greet new dogs, but most of the show owners appeared protective of their dogs.

Shelbee smiled. "That gives me a good reason to talk

to Colby. I'll tell her about Carolyn looking for her and find out what happened with Connors."

Bruce agreed. "That'll work for me too with Matt."

I wiped Paw's mouth with a napkin. "I wonder if Colby is who Matt went to call after we talked to him this morning. He didn't seem to know about Connors's death until we told him."

Bruce picked up his last fries. "Maybe. Could be he killed Connors or Colby did. Both had a motive."

Shelbee shook her head. "I thought you were sure Hoffman murdered Connors."

"He's still my chief suspect but from what we have learned Connors had a lot of enemies."

The waitress came to see if we needed anything.

Bruce gestured to his cup. "Can I get a coffee to go?"

"Sure. Do you ladies need anything?"

"No. Thank you."

We finished the rest of our meal quickly. The cafe had filled up while we had been eating.

Refusing money from Shelbee or me, Bruce waved us on. "I'll pay the tab. You guys go ahead."

We left the cafe and returned to the hall. Once in the hall, we separated with Paw going with Shelbee.

We agreed to meet back at Paw's assigned stall in an hour.

CHAPTER 6

$\mathcal{I}$ walked through the aisles of show dogs, heading for the mastiff section. It was less crowded now which I assumed was because of the lunch hour. The judges had taken a lunch break, so no judging was happening. I assumed that most of the spectators were away eating lunch as well. A few spectators were taking advantage of the lull to enjoy looking at the show dogs. Many owners had opted to eat their lunches in their stalls.

I found Hoffman in his stall feeding his mastiff. Both man and dog looked up as I stopped by their stall.

Hoffman frowned at me. I expected him to ask what I wanted in a growl, but instead, he said, "Can I help you?"

I held out my hand. "Clarissa Brantford. I wanted to compliment you on how well your dog is trained."

He shook my hand. "It takes discipline and hard work."

"Do you mind if I ask how you do it? You see, I have a Saint Bernard that doesn't listen well. I want to get him better trained."

"You have to show him that you are the boss. Dogs are pack animals. They follow the leader or alpha dog. You have to show them you are the alpha. I offer training courses. Here is a brochure."

He handed me the paper.

"Thank you. I'll consider it. I was truly impressed with how your dog stayed still when the terrier ran through the judging ring."

He smirked, and I had to bite my cheek to keep my face from showing disgust. "Amateurs who can't control their dogs don't belong in the ring."

"Do you have any idea how that dog got in the ring?"

"I have an idea, and that person will pay for it."

I waited for him to say more, but he didn't.

"How? Will you report them to the judging committee?"

"That's none of your concern."

I noticed that he hadn't bothered to introduce me to his dog. "What's your mastiff's name?"

"Samuel Van Brook. He's the best mastiff you will see at this show."

The dog looked up to Hoffman in adoration.

"And yet he didn't win the judging, why do you think that is?"

Hoffman's face turned red. "That judge is a disgrace to the ring. He chose purely to appease an old woman. I assure you I have put in a complaint and will see him banned and the judgment overturned."

I asked with a touch of awe in my voice, "Does that happen a lot? Bad judges?"

"More than it should."

"I'm sorry to hear that. Someone told me that you were part of the top show winners, along with Dorothy Hawkins, her husband, and Lyon Connors."

"Connors was a fraud. He would pull any trick to get an advantage in the judging."

"Didn't he accuse you of trying to drug his dog for a Best in Show competition?"

"He did. He was wrong. He had no proof, and the officials said as much. You sure are nosy. Just who are you?"

I smiled. "Just a concerned fellow dog owner."

He grunted, "Nosy dog owner."

"I like to know what's going on around me. In fact, I heard Connors's death was suspicious. Some people think he was murdered. What do you think?"

I was hoping for some sign of guilt.

Hoffman's expression remained blank. "Wouldn't surprise me."

"Would you have any idea who could have done it?"

"No. I don't. Why don't you ask Dorothy?"

"Why Dorothy?"

"She was the closest of the owners to Connors." He sneered. "Can't ask her husband, now can you?"

"You don't sound like you liked her husband."

"I didn't," he replied. "He pulled dirty tricks, just like

Connors. If Fred Hawkins weren't dead, I would say he killed Connors."

I was confused. "I thought Connors and Fred Hawkins were friends."

"Looked like it, but they were always competing aggressively against each other. Who's to say it didn't go too far? Fred was there when Connors accused me of trying to drug his dog. He could have been the one to drug the dog treat then retrieve it when Connors and I got into a fight."

"That certainly would clear you of wrongdoing."

His face reddened. "I'm done talking to you. Get out of here, and if I were you, I'd be careful asking so many questions."

His mastiff, Samuel, had stood and gone on alert at his master's change in tone.

Keeping an eye on the mastiff, I asked, "Is that a threat?"

"Consider it a warning."

He turned away, tugging on Samuel's leash to step back into his stall.

I left them, walking on down the aisle. I waved to Alex who was brushing Manny, but I had too much to think about to stop and talk.

Hoffman was certainly an aggressive and arrogant person. I could easily see him drugging Connors's dog. I could, also, see him killing Connors in a fit of anger. Seeing Alex reminded me of his comment about the loose dog. I could see Hoffman arranging that to win a competition. But Connors's death was planned and subtle, calculated to my way of thinking. Hoffman seemed more the kind of person to kill in a fit of temper.

What about Dorothy's husband? He may have tried to destroy Connors's chances of winning, but he was dead before Connors died. Did Connors have something to do with Dorothy's husband's death? Could Dorothy have taken revenge on Connors? I would have to question her and see if I could find more information about her husband's death.

It seemed I was getting more suspects and questions than answers. I had a lot to discuss with Bruce and Shelbee. Hopefully, they had more luck.

I made my way back to Paw's stall to wait for them.

Once there it occurred to me that it would be the perfect time to search Hoffman's room. He seemed settled in his stall for now. Maybe I would find something in his room that would incriminate him in Connors's death. I left my stall and headed to one of the side doors of the hall. From there I walked down a deserted corridor until I reached a stairwell, climbing to the second floor to my room. I didn't know which room was Hoffman's. Bruce had told me it was next door to our room, but I wasn't sure which side he'd meant. I figured he had written the room number down in his case folder as he kept meticulous notes on his cases.

I entered our room. It didn't take long to find the room number in Bruce's folder. I borrowed Bruce's lock picking kit as well. I wasn't sure I would be able to pick the lock, but Bruce had taught me some of the techniques for opening a door.

I left our room, closing the door behind me while I looked down the hall.

No one was in sight.

I turned right walking away from our room and the elevators and stopped at Hoffman's door.

I glanced around again.

Still no one in sight.

Opening the kit, I extracted one of the picks. Leaving the kit on the floor, I inserted the pick in the lock and wiggled it, trying to find a way to trip the lock open. Realizing that I needed another pick, I pulled out a second one and inserted it next to the first.

Engrossed in my task, I barely heard the elevator beep indicating it had stopped at our floor. Any second and the doors would open.

I frantically wiggled at the lock. It continued to resist my efforts.

By now I was sweating, and my hands were shaking, which didn't help with the lock picking. I debated giving up on the door and walking away, but I was so close to succeeding. I didn't know if I would get another opportunity to search Hoffman's room again.

Just as the elevator doors began to open, I felt the lock give.

I shoved open the door and rushed into the room, kicking the lock kit inside then closing the door quickly.

I stood with my back to the door, panting from anxiety and excitement.

I stopped breathing when I realized that it could be Hoffman returning to his room. What would I do if he was the one on the elevator? How would I get out?

I stuck the picks back in the case and let it lie on the floor next to the door.

I took a deep breath, put my ear to the door, and listened.

I heard footsteps and an odd rolling sound.

I stretched up and peeked through the peephole.

Two women dressed in white uniforms were walking past the door pushing a cart. Housekeeping. They continued to the end of the hall, each one entering a room at the end, on opposite sides of the hallway.

I breathed a sigh of relief.

I didn't know how long it would take them to clean so I figured I had better hurry and search the room.

Hoffman's room was the same as ours except he didn't have a couch. The room appeared slightly smaller but had the same color scheme as ours.

Directly across from the door was the bed with a nightstand on one side. Hoffman appeared to be a tidy person. Unlike our room, his bed was neatly made. I had tried to straighten the bedspread in our room with Paw's enthusiastic help. The results were not impressive.

A chest of drawers stood on the left-hand wall with a

closed door next to it. Based on our room, I assumed it was the closet. A table and two chairs sat between the bed and closet. The table was bare. To my right another door stood open, revealing the bathroom.

I walked to the nightstand and used my shirt tail to pull open the top drawer. Inside was a Bible and pack of tissues.

The bottom drawer of the nightstand was empty. I moved to the chest of drawers. On top lay a hairbrush with a few strands of dark brown hair stuck in the teeth. They matched Hoffman's hair color. A pack of mint-flavored gum lay beside the brush.

A red choker dog collar with a leash was on the dresser top as well.

I cringed at the sight of it. I couldn't stand the thought of this type of collar being used on any dog. I certainly wouldn't use one on Paw and I knew Shelbee had had to lecture a few of her dog owners about not using them.

Hoffman seemed like the controlling owner who wouldn't think twice about using it.

I opened the top drawer to find it filled with under-wear. I sighed in frustration. Pawing through the man's underwear seemed too invasive, but I gingerly moved the items from one side to the other to see if anything else was there.

Nothing.

As I closed the drawer, it occurred to me that I should check for anything tape to the tops or sides of drawers.

At least, that is what happened in old movies. I reopened the drawer and checked.

Nothing.

I proceeded to check the next two drawers. All I found were T-shirts, socks, and belts. I rechecked the nightstand drawers for any hidden items but found nothing.

I was running out of time. I peeked through the peephole but didn't see anything. I could hear the cleaning cart squeak as it moved down the hallway. I still had time to continue searching.

The closet was next. Two suitcases sat on the floor and jackets and pants hung on the hangers. I checked the pockets and linings of the coats and the pockets on the pants. Again, nothing. One suitcase felt empty when I lifted it. It was made of brown leather and had a brass lock. I was relieved to discover the lock had the key in it. Presumably, there was nothing of value inside, or he would have locked it. Still, I did a search. The satin lining felt smooth, and I couldn't find any bulges or hidden places.

I put the brown suitcase back and tugged on its mate. Both suitcases were identical except that this one was heavy. I dragged it out of the closet. Once again, the key was in the lock. I turned the key and lifted the lid. Inside was a variety of pet supplies and dog training equipment. I emptied the entire case trying to memorize where everything was placed so I could put it back the same way. There were dog treats and chew toys. I found another leash and dog collar. This collar was a standard leather one in black. A dog grooming kit contained brushes and shampoo. Most of the training equipment was foreign to me. I only vaguely recognized some of it from Shelbee's descriptions of tools she used. Everything looked like your typical dog paraphernalia. I set it aside and felt the lining. No bulges or hidden pockets. I carefully returned everything, vowing to describe the items to Shelbee to confirm they were normal equipment. I shoved the suitcase back into the closet and shut the door.

I didn't have much time left. I could hear the cleaning ladies talking close by, then sounds of a vacuum running next door. I headed to the bathroom.

Passing the bed, I realized I hadn't searched it, but decided to check the bathroom first.

I wished Paw were here with me. He was great at finding clues.

Everything in the bathroom looked neat and in place. On the sink sat a shaving kit. I opened it surprised to find more than a razor and soap inside. Hoffman had several pill bottles as well.

I studied the bottles.

By now, I was sweating again because I could hear the cleaning ladies in the room next door. The first two pill bottles contained heartburn medication and high blood pressure pills. The third one I didn't recognize. Something about it nagged me.

I didn't have anything to write down the name, so I

MASTIFFS, MYSTERY, AND MURDER

opened the bottle and took out one of the pills while trying to memorize the name. I hoped I could remember it.

The vacuuming ceased next door. The cleaning women were in the same room now, finishing the last of their tasks.

I re-closed the lid to the pill bottle and stuffed it into the bag. I zipped the kit and hurried out of the bathroom, stuffing the pill into my pants pocket.

Going to the door, I peeked through the peephole. I felt like I was becoming a regular peeping tom. No one was in sight, so I cautiously opened the door a crack. I could hear the cleaning crew just inside the door beside me. The rest of the hallway was clear. I locked the door and quietly shut it.

I scurried down the hall to my room and thrust my key in the lock.

The elevator door dinged and began to open.

I rushed into my room and quickly shut the door, throwing my back against it. Whew! I'd done it. I didn't know how Bruce managed to be a private detective. I was stressed from my snooping.

That was the moment I realized that I had messed up.

I'd left the lock picking kit on the floor in Hoffman's room.

Oh no. Now what?

CHAPTER 7

*H*ow could I have been so stupid?

Standing here wasn't going to solve the problem. I turned around and eased open the door. Out in the hall, I heard footsteps coming from the elevator.

I peeked in that direction and gasped.

Hoffman strode down the hall toward me.

The cleaning ladies were at his room door. One sorted items on their cart while the other turned toward Hoffman's door, preparing to insert her master key.

Hoffman called to the maids, "I don't want you going in there."

The maids turned to look at him. "Is this your room?" the one with the key asked.

"Yes."

Shoot, now what was I going to do?

The elevator bell dinged again, the door opened, and a

tall man with graying hair stepped out. He wore one of the dog show badges denoting an official of the show. He strode forward, saying, "Mr. Hoffman, I need to speak with you."

Hoffman turned. "I'll talk with you in the hall in a few minutes." He turned away from the official as if dismissing him.

The official spoke again, "Now, Mr. Hoffman. There has been a serious complaint lodged against you. We need to clear this up."

"What!" Hoffman whirled around to face the official. "That is ridiculous!"

"Nevertheless, you need to come with me immediately."

"Fine. I'm coming." He waved at the cleaning ladies. "Go ahead and clean my room."

Both men returned to the elevator. As soon as the doors closed, I stepped out of my room. One of the ladies had already opened Hoffman's door and stepped inside. The other had entered the room across the hall.

I tiptoed to Hoffman's door and saw the maid carrying an armful of towels. She headed into the bathroom. Fortunately, she hadn't seen the kit to the right side of the doorway.

I reached around and grabbed the kit then scurried back to my room before either of the maids saw me. I returned Bruce's kit to his suitcase then peeked out the door.

Both maids were still in their rooms. I locked our door and rushed to the stairwell next to the elevator. I didn't want the maids to see me, even though it probably didn't matter. I didn't want anyone to find me on that floor. I took the stairs down to the main floor, out of breath by the time I reached the bottom. I needed to get more exercise as Shelbee kept telling me.

I returned to the hall and went to my stall. I was expecting that both Shelbee and Bruce would be there by now, so I was surprised to find the stall empty. I sat down and took a few minutes to relax and consider what I had learned. What kind of complaint had been lodged against Hoffman? Who complained? I needed to find out more information, but who could I ask?

Shelbee came down the aisle swinging her arms and smiling.

I grinned. "You look happy. Does that mean you had success?"

"Yes, I did." She stepped into the stall and sat on a folding chair next to mine.

The chairs were standard issue metal that always seemed to hurt my back and butt if I sat in them too long. I hadn't taken the time to find a cushion to pad the chair.

I frowned. "Where's Paw?"

"He's with Bruce. Matt left his stall as we neared it, so

Bruce followed him, taking Paw. Bruce claimed he'd look less suspicious walking a dog."

"I hope they get back soon. Paw doesn't always listen too well, and he's not used to Bruce walking him."

"Stop worrying," Shelbee said. "Paw will be fine. He can take care of himself and Bruce too."

"Tell me about your talk with Colby. Did you find out anything?"

"Not much. She was evasive with most of her answers. She was happy to know that Carolyn was looking for her and willing to talk about dogs in general. When I mentioned that I was a pet sitter, she became anxious."

"How do you mean?"

"She darted glances around the hall and wrung her hands. It was as if she didn't want anyone to remember that she had been a pet sitter."

I shifted in my chair. "Carolyn said she was the best pet sitter she ever had."

"Exactly. Whatever happened with Connors must have devastated her. I couldn't get her to answer any questions and the more I asked, the more anxious she became. When I mentioned Connors, she visibly paled and wouldn't talk anymore. Then she asked me to leave because she had to get one of the Chihuahuas ready for the ring. The Toy Group judging is this afternoon."

"Did one of Matt's dogs qualify for group judging?"

"Yes, Lila won. She'll compete in the group competi-

tion this afternoon against the other winning breeds in the Toy Group. If she wins her group, she'll compete in the Best in Show tomorrow. Did you talk to Hoffman?"

"Yes. He denied any wrongdoing, says he never drugged Connors's dog. He inferred that Dorothy's husband could have drugged the dog. Plus, he claims he knows who put the loose dog in the ring earlier today."

Shelbee raised her eyebrows. "Do you believe him?"

"I believe he knows who ruined the competition today. Do you think Dorothy or her husband could have been the ones to drug Connors's dog?"

"I suppose it's possible. Most people like Dorothy well enough. She can be a bit opinionated and exacting, but she truly loves the dogs. Owners respect that so I wouldn't think Dorothy would drug another dog. Her husband wasn't as well respected. He was more like Connors which may be why they were friends. I can see Fred doing something like that. Win at any cost."

"Sounds like Hoffman was right. Fred Hawkins would have been the perfect suspect in Connors's death if not for the fact he was already dead. I'm going to have to talk to Dorothy about this."

"Better wait until this evening. She is in the group competitions this afternoon. Her Pomeranian won its breed category, so they are in the Toy Group too. Dorothy won't talk to you when she's in show mode."

I nodded in agreement then lowered my voice. "I wanted to show you something I found." I pulled out the pill I had found in Hoffman's room and quietly explained how I found it.

Shelbee's eyes widened, but she didn't say anything until I had finished. "I can't believe you did that. You're lucky you didn't get caught."

"I know, but it was too good an opportunity to pass up."

"Are you going to tell Bruce?"

I sighed. "Yes, but I am not looking forward to that conversation. He's going to be furious, never mind that he would have done the same thing."

Shelbee smiled. "It's true, but he'll remind you that he has a license to investigate."

"Isn't that the truth? Of course, I'm not sure that his license covers sneaking into someone else's room and searching." I pointed to the pill. "Do you have any idea what that is?"

Shelbee's smile faded. "I'm not sure, but I know who to ask. Sal is a friend, and he's here at the show."

"When can we talk to him?"

"How about right now?" Shelbee stood up. "We'll go to his vendor stand. Sal used to be a veterinarian but gave up his practice a few years ago. Now he sells a line of naturopathic herbs, medicines, and accessories to pet owners who want an alternative to traditional medicines for their pets."

Shelbee and I walked through the hall where dog fanciers were bustling to and from the rings.

I raised an eyebrow at all the activity.

Shelbee explained, "The Best in Group judging is starting soon."

I saw Dorothy carrying her dog toward one of the rings trailed by an owner with a Bichon Frise in her arms. The Toy Group must have been the next group in judging.

Just then, over the loudspeaker, a voice announced, "Ten minutes until the Toy Group judging."

Shelbee and I turned right at the end of the aisle and proceeded to the area designated for the vendors. All types of products and services were represented here. Dog grooming supplies, bathing services, dog-themed merchandise and even a pet psychic were available for the right price. I saw a beautiful tote bag with a Saint Bernard pictured on it. Tempting. I hesitated to check the price since funds were a little tight this month. It takes a lot to feed Paw, and my writing income can be erratic.

Shelbee led me to Sal's stand. His booth was one stall in from one of the side doors to the hall. On the side nearest the door was a stand selling premium dog food. The stand on Sal's other side was selling pet portraits. The artist had several portraits on display. Her work was outstanding. I sighed, thinking about how nice it would be to have a portrait of Paw. Sal wasn't at his stand, but Shelbee introduced me to his assistant, and girlfriend, Rebecca.

Shelbee smiled at Rebecca. "I had a question for Sal. Any idea when he'll be back?"

Rebecca was a tall woman with thin cheeks and long,

braided hair. She wore a shift-style dress and reminded me of a hippie with the beads around her neck. "He went to consult on a Weimaraner's diet. He'll be gone for a while. I don't expect him back for at least an hour. The owner's demanding if you know what I mean." She giggled in a high-pitched voice.

Shelbee's strained smile told me the laugh was as annoying to her as to me. "Well, maybe I could catch up with him. Do you know which owner it is?"

Rebecca's eyes widened. "I can't tell you that." She sounded truly scandalized. "Client privilege and all that." She nodded her head decisively.

Shelbee sighed. "Then I'll catch him this evening sometime."

She emitted another high-pitched giggle. "He won't be here. He has to go back home to pick up more supplies. We're selling out of calming herbs like crazy!"

I could hear Shelbee gritting her teeth. "All right. Please just let him know I stopped by and need to talk to him."

"I can do that. What's your name again?"

I left Shelbee to finish with Rebecca and stepped over to the portrait artist. She smiled warmly at me.

The artist was a small woman with curly, light brown hair. Her green eyes sparkled behind her wire-framed glasses. She sat at a small table which displayed a partially finished drawing that she was coloring.

I admired her work. "Mind if I observe?"

"I don't mind at all." She had a low, cultured voice.

I watched her draw for several minutes. She was using colored pencils to render a likeness of a Great Dane from photos she had positioned at the top of her work table. Shelbee quietly joined me. She, too, seemed fascinated by the artist's talent. The Great Dane was coming alive on her canvas.

I said, "You do beautiful work. I can't even draw a stick figure."

She smiled at that while Shelbee shook her head in agreement.

"Clarissa is right. You are talented, and she can't even draw a stick figure."

I gave Shelbee a friendly push.

Shelbee watched the woman work. "Do you get many commissions at a show like this?"

"Yes. Quite a few. I have done well at this show. Would you like to have one done?"

I thought of Paw. "I would love to, but unfortunately, I don't have the money right now to get one done. Besides, I have a Saint Bernard. He is not the cooperative type for a portrait."

She smiled. "I only work from photos you provide of your pet. He doesn't have to sit for a portrait. Many animals are too lively for that kind of thing."

She reached behind her and handed me a card. "My name is Pamela Wright. That is my business card. I'd be happy to do a portrait in the future. With so many commissions at this show, it will be six months before I could deliver a portrait even if you ordered today."

"That's okay. It will take me six months to get good photos of Paw. Thank you."

She nodded and resumed coloring.

I asked Shelbee, "Did you find out when you can see Sal?"

Shelbee grimaced. "Sometime tomorrow. My guess would be late morning."

I nodded.

We had just entered the aisle with Paw's stall when I spotted my playful Saint Bernard running toward me. For a minute, I stood still in surprise. Paw was dragging our friend, Jacqueline, behind him. Where was Bruce? Then I saw him trailing behind Jac.

Jacqueline Marie Weldon was my other best friend. She, Shelbee, and I had been close friends since we were kids. Jac was of medium height with beautiful black hair and stunning blue eyes.

I was delighted to see her.

Paw and Jac reached us and Paw jumped up on me.

Shelbee reached out and gave Jac a hug.

As I hugged Paw, I heard Shelbee ask Jac, "How'd you get here?"

Paw's tongue lolled out in a happy grin. Both Jac and Shelbee were getting whipped by his huge waving tail.

Jac laughed. "I was in the area shopping when Paw found me."

I looked over at Bruce who blushed.

Jac continued. "I had just come out of the bakery on Fulsom when Paw rushed up to me, trailing his leash. I looked for you, then saw Bruce."

No wonder Bruce was blushing. Paw had gotten away from him. I wasn't the only one who had trouble keeping Paw to heel.

I asked Bruce, "What were you doing on Fulsom?"

"I..." Bruce began but stopped at the excited chatter surrounding us.

We were standing in the middle of the aisle, and people had been flowing around us. Now everyone seemed to be talking about the same thing.

"A tie! I can't believe it."

"That hasn't happened since..."

"Which breeds?"

"The Pomeranian and the Chihuahua."

"I thought sure Dorothy would win."

Shelbee stopped a passing woman. "Hey, Gladys, what's all the excitement?"

Gladys was a middle-aged Asian woman carrying a toy poodle. "The judge declared a tie in the Toy Group. The Pomeranian and the Chihuahua. It hasn't happened in ages. Dorothy almost always wins her group."

I asked, "What happens next?"

"They both compete in the Best in Show," she said then hurried away.

Shelbee gazed after Gladys. "Hmm. That won't make the others in Best in Show happy. More competition."

Bruce was shaking his head. "I don't understand. Matt was just on Fulsom Street. I followed him to a pet store and was waiting for him to come out when Paw bolted to meet Jac. How could he have returned so fast and competed?"

Shelbee reminded Bruce, "He doesn't have to be the one in the ring. He can have someone else show his dog."

"Then who did show the Chihuahua?"

Jac nudged Shelbee. "Go ask someone."

Shelbee looked around and waved to a woman I recognized. It was Patricia, the dachshund owner, who had been consulting Shelbee earlier in the day. Shelbee left us and went to talk to Patricia. She was back within minutes. "Colby showed the dog."

Bruce, Shelbee, and I stood thinking.

Jac sighed. "Okay guys, what's really going on? I know Shelbee is into these shows, but what's up with you two?"

We all shushed her.

Bruce said, "Let's go somewhere private to talk."

My stomach grumbled. "Why don't we go to our hotel room and order room service? I'm starving again."

Paw woofed at my suggestion. He was hungry too.

Jac's eyes had widened at the mention of a hotel room, and she winked at me.

I had some explaining to do before she got the wrong idea.

We all agreed room service was a good idea.

As we walked to the elevators and rode up to our floor, I knew I had a lot to explain to Bruce as well. I wasn't sure how he would feel about me searching Hoffman's room. I had a feeling I was going to be in trouble big time. Never mind that he would have done the same thing.

CHAPTER 8

*O*ur floor was empty when the elevators opened, but that wouldn't last long. The Toy Group judging had been the last group of the day. The rest of the groups would compete tomorrow morning, and the Best in Show competition would happen in the afternoon. The dog show would be closing about now, and the spectators and visitors would be heading home. The owners would be settling their dogs for the night in their hotel rooms. A few may leave their dogs in their stalls in the hall, but most seemed to want their pets with them. I know I did.

As soon as I opened our hotel door, Paw walked to the bed and jumped up on it. He turned around three times and settled down in the middle of the bed.

Jac and Shelbee laughed at him, and Bruce smiled.

Bruce dug out the menu from under the phone. "What's everybody want to eat?"

We took several minutes to study and debate our dining options.

I chose roasted chicken breast with rice and carrots. Plus, I ordered a second plain chicken breast for Paw. I had his food with me, but I knew he would expect to eat some people food too.

Shelbee and Jac were still debating food choices while Bruce had decided on steak.

I decided to feed Paw before our food arrived. I went into the bathroom and cleaned and refreshed his water bowl. I'd left it in the bathroom since it had a tile floor and Paw often got water everywhere when he drank. I collected his food dish and washed it out then left the bathroom with it to open the closet with his canned food.

Up to now, Paw had been blissfully sleeping on the bed. As I opened the closet door, I peeked at him. One eye had partially opened.

I unzipped the suitcase where I kept his food, pulled out a can and opener, and re-zipped the case.

Turning with the can, I spied a wide-awake Paw sitting up, staring at me. He jumped off the bed and rushed over to me, waving his tail joyously as I opened his food.

I dumped his food in his bowl and carried it to the bathroom.

He followed me then eagerly began to eat.

I left him at it and went back to join the others after disposing of the empty can in the trash and putting away the opener.

Bruce had finished phoning in the order. It would be about twenty minutes until our food arrived.

Jac sat on the settee. "All right. Now tell me what is going on. Why are you at a dog show?"

I sat down next to her. "Paw was competing in the Saint Bernard category."

Jac's mouth fell open.

I couldn't help laughing at her expression. I would have had the same reaction a few days ago if anyone had told me Paw would be in competition. My lovable mutt was certainly a purebred dog, but he didn't behave like a show dog. Rough and tumble would be better descriptions.

"I think it would be best if we started at the beginning."

Jac nodded in agreement.

I nodded to Bruce. "I'll let you explain."

Paw finished his meal and settled at my feet.

Bruce began with the death of Connors and the need to be part of the show which was how Paw and I got involved. He explained everything up to the point where he separated from us after lunch.

Jac had lots of questions. She loved a mystery as much as the rest of us did. Besides, Jac had helped in many former investigations, including the case involving her missing aunt.

A knock sounded on the door. Room service had arrived.

Paw went charging to the door.

I hurried to Paw and grabbed his collar.

Shelbee and I pulled him into the bathroom so that room service could safely deliver. Paw wouldn't have hurt the service person, but he easily could have jumped up at the food on the cart.

Bruce knocked on the bathroom door after the hotel staff left. Jac had cut Paw's chicken breast up on a piece of aluminum foil, and now she placed it on the floor as we led Paw out. He trotted to her and set to eating.

Jac handed out plates, and we went to eating. The first few minutes were spent savoring our meals. Paw begged a little at first, but soon settled back on the bed and went to sleep with a sigh. I spoiled him but had managed to train him not beg at the table.

I cut up my chicken. "What happened when you followed Matt?"

"Nothing. Like I said before, he went to the pet store, and I waited outside. I didn't want to be too obvious following him. I doubted he was doing anything suspicious at a pet store. I was going to go in after him when Paw saw Jac and took off. I'm sure he was tired of standing around doing nothing for a half hour."

Jac swallowed. "That's how long he was in the pet store?"

"Yeah. I wondered if Matt spotted me and slipped out the back. I watched through the window for the first fifteen minutes then he walked to the back of the store, and I couldn't see him. I should have realized no one spends that much time shopping for pet stuff."

Shelbee and I smiled at each other.

"What?"

Jac explained, "Clarissa can spend hours in a pet store looking at dog supplies and toys. It's the one place she loves to shop."

Shelbee picked up her fork. "Most pet owners are the same way. Matt was probably just shopping."

Bruce shrugged. He asked Shelbee and me, "How did you two do while Paw and I were gone?"

Shelbee took a sip of tea. "I didn't get any information out of Matt's girlfriend." She told Bruce and Jac about her conversation with Colby.

I finished my carrots. "Connors must have really hurt Colby's career. I wonder why?"

Bruce said, "You're assuming that Connors was the only one who complained."

Something niggled at the back of my brain, but then disappeared. *What was I forgetting?*

"True, but we do know of at least one person who felt Colby did an excellent job." I explained to Jac about meeting Carolyn at the hotel cafe. "Carolyn seemed a smart and dedicated owner. I don't think she would have hired someone who was negligent."

Shelbee nodded. "I agree."

Bruce had to agree as well. He looked at me. "What about you? How did your conversation with Hoffman go?"

I recounted the conversation. Bruce scowled the more

I told him. "I want you to stay away from him. I don't like that he threatened you."

"I wouldn't call it a threat. More like a warning."

Jac set her napkin on the table. "Do you think Hoffman let that dog loose in the ring?"

"Maybe, if so, it didn't work to his advantage in the end. So now he put in a complaint against the judge." I turned to look at Shelbee. "Do you think the officials will change the judge's decision?"

"I doubt it. Most decisions stand. Besides, if Connor complains too much, the judges may discover his part in the loose dog. That is if he was responsible."

"Aha," I said. Everyone looked at me. "I finally remembered what's been bothering me. Someone put in a complaint against Hoffman."

"Where did you hear that?"

I realized I hadn't told her about the conversation between Hoffman and the dog show official. Plus, I hadn't confessed to Bruce about borrowing his tools and breaking into Hoffman's room.

I hesitated. "It was after I searched Hoffman's room and was hiding in our room."

Bruce threw down his napkin. "What! What were you thinking?"

I gritted my teeth. "I thought that I had the perfect opportunity to look for any evidence of Hoffman's connection to Connors's death. He was busy in the hall. No one was around the rooms at that time of day, except the maids."

"The maids. How did you convince one of them to unlock Hoffman's door?"

"I didn't. I have a confession to make. I borrowed your lock picks to open the door."

"You did what! Breaking into a room is a crime."

"You do it."

Bruce growled. "I'm a private investigator. I know the risks."

"So do I. Besides, you're the one who taught me how to pick a lock."

Bruce grunted.

Paw had come to stand beside me, leaning on my leg. He hated when I raised my voice. If a dog could glare, Paw was glaring at Bruce.

"I returned the picks to your case."

Bruce grunted again and stalked to the closet to check his picks.

Shelbee and Jac had been quiet.

In the new silence, I could hear a dog next door whining.

Jac looked pointedly at Bruce. "Why don't you tell us what did happen and we'll all listen quietly."

Bruce scowled back, but came over, and folding his arms across his chest, stood silently watching me.

Sighing, I recounted my search of Hoffman's room and my findings.

Bruce's scowl deepened the longer I talked. "Let's see this pill."

Shelbee dug it out of her pocket and handed it to Bruce.

I noticed Paw had left my side to go to the hotel room door. He stood with his head cocked to the side, listening. I realized the dog next door was still whining. I silently promised Paw we would go soon for a pre-bedtime walk.

Bruce examined the pill. "You think this could be important?"

I turned from looking at Paw to answer Bruce. "I don't know, but with all the rumors and accusations about sabotaged dogs, I thought it might be important."

Jac began to gather the plates. "What about the other pills you saw?"

"I recognized them. Unless the pills were counterfeit, they looked to be a common antacid and high blood pressure medicine. My uncle takes both. It was only this pill that I wasn't familiar with."

Bruce knew my uncle since he was the chief of police of our small town. Bruce had worked with him on past cases.

Jac turned to Shelbee. "Could either of those medicines be used on a dog to knock him out of the competition?"

"I don't know for sure, but I can ask Sal when I talk to him tomorrow. It makes me so angry to know that dog owners would stoop so low to win a competition."

Jac stacked the plates on the room service cart. "Could there be another reason Hoffman wanted Connors dead?"

Bruce thought a moment. "Could be but the man kept to himself except for these shows."

Shelbee gasped. "What if these pills had something to do with Connors's death?"

I was stunned. "I hadn't considered the pills in connection with Connors's death. It's frightening to think that Hoffman may have brought a murder weapon with him to use on another dog fancier."

Bruce held up a hand. "Let's not jump to conclusions. These pills may have nothing to do with our case. But I'll spend more time watching Hoffman."

Shelbee nodded. "We all should. I don't want him to harm any of the dogs."

Jac and I nodded in agreement.

Bruce continued. "Then let's plan out how we will watch Hoffman."

Paw whined and dug at the door.

Next door, Hoffman's mastiff was howling in distress.

Shelbee jumped up. "He needs help."

Paw was barking and howling in earnest too.

Shelbee was heading to the door with Jac and me on her heels.

Bruce strode past us. "Wait. I'll go first."

I grasped Paw's collar so he wouldn't bolt from the room.

Bruce opened the door and began to step into the hallway. He had to stop to let two men pass. One wore a hotel security uniform while the other wore a suit.

The suited man, short with thinning hair, motioned to

us. "It's okay, folks. We have this handled. You can go back to your rooms."

We weren't the only ones whose door was open. Across the hall, Matt had his head and shoulders stuck out of his door. Further down the hall, three other dog owners were stepping out of their rooms.

Matt looked across at us and said, "Colby was worried, so I called down to the night desk."

We nodded in understanding. Considering the argument Matt had had with Hoffman, I couldn't blame him for not wanting to knock on the man's door. At least he thought enough of the mastiff to call for help.

The suited man knocked on Hoffman's door. "Mr. Hoffman. I am the night manager. Please open up. We need your dog to stop barking."

He continued to knock, sounding more frustrated and less polite. "Open up, or I will be forced to come in."

The mastiff was digging at the door and barking frantically.

Paw was pulling against my hold on his collar and barking as well.

Several other dogs were beginning to bark in commiseration, including Matt's Chihuahuas, who were yipping in his room.

I shushed Paw, but he was upset by the mastiff's plight.

The hotel manager pounded on the door. "Mr. Hoffman. Open up!"

I doubted Hoffman could hear the manager with all

the noise the dogs were making.

The manager handed his keys to the guard. "Open it."

The guard stepped to the door, inserted the key, turned it, and pushed at the door. At first, the door wouldn't budge because of the mastiff's body pressed against it. Once a little room appeared, the mastiff stuck his head and shoulders through and bolted out of the room.

He barreled into the guard who reeled into the hotel manager taking both men to the ground in an ungainly heap.

Bruce attempted to grab the mastiff, but he clipped Bruce in the shin sending him falling into me.

I lost my grip on Paw's collar, and he jerked from my grasp. I landed on the hall floor with Bruce on top of me.

Oomph! My breath rushed out of me. As I tried to sit up, one of Matt's Chihuahuas raced past me, chasing after Paw and the mastiff.

I turned in time to see the dogs reach the elevator.

By now, the guard and manager had risen to their feet, and Matt had stumbled out of his room. But Bruce and I were still half-lying in the middle of the hallway.

Shelbee and Jac were trapped in our hotel room by Bruce's and my legs.

Bruce and I scurried to our feet in time to the ping of the elevator arriving.

The elevator doors opened, and I breathed a sigh of relief that no one was in it.

Who knew what the mastiff would do in his frantic

state?

The night manager and guard along with Matt and Bruce started running to the elevators. It looked like they were going to be able to corner the dogs safely. I assumed Paw was going to try to stop the mastiff from getting away.

Imagine my surprise when Paw barked and led the dogs into the elevator.

I stood in shock. I didn't know what Paw thought he was doing. It looked, though, like the guys were still going to be able to catch them.

Then Paw gave me a pointed look as if to say "follow me" and jumped up, hitting the inside panel of buttons on the elevator.

The doors closed a second before the guys reached them.

The indicator light's down arrow turned green, and the elevator began its descent.

Had Paw meant to do that?

All four men said some choice curse words then turned to the stairwell door.

Bruce and the guard jostled each other to be the first through the door. They got stuck in the doorway. The hotel manager and Matt were pushing from behind. After some wriggling and more curse words, Bruce got through first with the other three men following right behind him.

Shelbee raced ahead with Jac right behind her. "Come on."

I ran after them and through the stairwell door. Everyone soon outdistanced me. Drat, these short legs of mine. Of course, it didn't help that I could stand to lose a few pounds and work out more.

Halfway down, I had to stop to take a rest for a minute. Catching my breath, I reached the bottom of the stairwell, exited through the door, and stopped, laughing at the scene before me.

Paw, the mastiff, and the Chihuahua were running back and forth through the foyer with Bruce, Matt, the guard, and the night manager following. The dogs' antics made the men look inept.

Bruce dashed around an end table after Paw, skidding on the polished floor. He windmilled his arms and just barely kept himself from falling.

Matt had crawled partway under a sofa to try to reach his dog. The Chihuahua, who I recognized as Lila, gave a yip and ran out the other side. She made a sharp U-turn and leaped on Matt's butt while Matt was still trying to back out from under the sofa. The dog kept its balance as Matt wiggled out then jumped off and ran toward Paw just as Matt emerged from under the sofa.

The night manager stood blocking the archway to the convention hall while the security guard tried to catch the mastiff.

The guard lunged to grab the mastiff, but he was a fraction too late in capturing him. The mastiff easily evaded his grasp. The guard, however, overbalanced in his lunge and went skidding face first across the floor.

I couldn't help it. I laughed out loud, noticing that I wasn't the only one.

Shelbee and Jac both wore grins. They had stopped about three feet to my right and were observing the scene.

Behind the check-in desk stood a young hotel clerk who was grinning as well. He laughed out loud when the guard slid across the floor. This earned him the attention of the manager.

"Get out here and help us," he ordered the young man.

The clerk scurried from behind the desk.

Paw and the Chihuahua were both frisking around the room. Both Bruce and Matt stood bent over with hands on their knees, catching their breath.

The mastiff, though, found himself in trouble. With the help of the clerk, the guard and manager had cornered the mastiff. The dog was baring its teeth and snarling. The guard had found a rope somewhere and was attempting to lasso the dog while the clerk and manager distracted him.

I was worried. This couldn't be good.

Shelbee felt the same way for she began to protest, "You can't do that."

The manager cut her off with a "Don't interfere." Then turned his attention back to the mastiff.

All three men had forgotten about Paw and the Chihuahua, to their detriment.

The guard had the rope lasso ready and was flicking his wrist to throw it.

At the last second, Paw body-slammed him to the ground.

I heard Jac say, "Ooh, that had to hurt."

Meanwhile, Lila had latched onto the pants leg of the manager who was shaking his foot, trying to dislodge the dog.

Matt ran to help Lila. "Hey. Leave my dog alone!"

The clerk backed off when he realized he was alone with the mastiff.

The dog rushed out through the archway toward the hall.

Paw jumped over the guard with a "woof" and a look back at me that clearly said, "Follow us."

The Chihuahua let go of the manager's pants leg and hurried after the other dogs.

I followed them with Shelbee and Jac right behind me.

The mastiff stopped at the main doors to the hall. He barked, howled, and scratched at the door, looking for a way to get in through the closed doors.

Paw looked back at me as I rushed up. He jumped up at the door and tried to turn the knob. If it had been a lever type knob, he would have opened it. Instead, the door had a standard rounded knob. Paw hadn't figured out how to open those kinds. Yet.

I cautiously pushed through the dogs to the door. I wasn't sure the mastiff would let me close to him without a growl, but he accepted my presence with no protest. I tried to turn the knob, but it was locked tight. The dogs continued to fuss.

I looked back at Shelbee and Jac. "It's locked tight."

Shelbee said, "They really want to get in there. We should help them."

Jac stared at the door. "But how?"

I sighed. "I don't know. Let me think."

Jac looked over her shoulder. "Better hurry up with that. The guys are coming."

As she said it, Bruce and Matt ran up to us.

"The doors are locked," I said. "We need more time."

Bruce nodded at Matt. "We'll try to hold the others back."

Matt was looking down at his dog and frowning. "I don't know about this..." he began, but Bruce clapped him on the shoulder and steered him back the way they had come. More footsteps could be heard in that direction. It sounded as if the manager had called in reinforcements.

Shelbee suggested, "There are other entrances. Why don't we try one of those?"

I turned to my right. "Good idea."

Jac asked, "Why that way?"

"The closest side entrance is down this hallway."

"Shouldn't we divide up and try other entrances?"

Shelbee shook her head. "No. I think Clarissa is right. Best to stick together."

The three of us walked down the hall to the side door.

The mastiff didn't want to follow, but Paw gave him a shove in our direction. I thought sure the mastiff would protest, but he went willingly. Lila happily followed along. We reached the side door and found it unlocked.

As soon as Shelbee opened the door, all three dogs rushed inside. The lights were off, and I had no idea where the switch was located. The dogs had no problems seeing with their excellent vision, though. All three disappeared into the darkness.

I called to Paw to come back, but he ignored me. I stood still trying to decide what to do.

Then I heard a chilling howl come from the mastiff. It was the most frightening and mournful sound I think I have ever heard.

I shivered, turning to Jac and Shelbee.

Jac stood with her arms wrapped around herself while Shelbee shifted from foot to foot, ready to rush to the mastiff's aid.

The lights suddenly came on, and I jumped. The light blinded me for a second.

To our left, Bruce, Matt, the manager, and two guards headed toward us. They were arguing amongst themselves.

Bruce reached my side and explained, "The manager opened the main door with his key."

I nodded.

The men behind him continued to bicker until the mastiff gave another mournful howl, followed by intense barking from Paw and Lila.

The men fell silent, bickering forgotten.

The mastiff howled again, then whimpered.

Bruce grasped my hand. "That doesn't sound good."

CHAPTER 9

Slowly we followed the sound of the mastiff's whimpering. Bruce and I were in the lead followed closely by Shelbee, Jac, and Matt. The side door the girls and I had entered from was about midway of the hall. We had turned right and we were continuing to walk down an aisle lined with stalls on both sides. The stalls appeared to be empty. I assumed most owners had taken their dogs to their hotel rooms.

The manager and his guards had chosen to take the next aisle to our left. They were walking parallel to us. I heard another yip. The dogs sounded as if they were at the end of the aisle, but I couldn't see them for the pile of boxes blocking it.

I pointed to the boxes. "That wasn't there earlier."

Bruce agreed. "Best go over to the next aisle."

Fortunately, we were close to a cross aisle and could turn left onto it. Then we turned right onto the aisle just ahead of the manager and his guards. We continued to the end of the aisle.

We turned right again into the end aisle where the vendors had their booths.

Shelbee gasped and pointed.

The dogs were gathered together at the stall that displayed a new version of dog food. Bags of food had spilled dog kibble across the floor.

Oddly, none of the dogs were eating the kibble.

Instead, they were standing over an object half buried in the piles of food and bags.

A body.

I gasped. "Oh no. Someone's lying there."

The mastiff gave another mournful howl as we rushed down the aisle.

A man was lying face down in the kibble with arms splayed out. Blood matted the dark brown hair of the victim's head. A flash of red caught my attention. A red choker dog collar was drawn tight around the victim's neck with the leash trailing down his back.

Suddenly, I knew who the victim was - Hoffman.

Bruce knelt to feel for a pulse.

The mastiff began to growl protectively.

Paw gently nudged the mastiff to calm him.

I had been so focused on the body that I had forgotten the dogs.

Paw and the Chihuahua were both pressing against the mastiff's side as if offering comfort. The mastiff calmed down and let Bruce check Hoffman's pulse.

Bruce stood up again and said to us, "Dead."

The hotel manager looked stricken. "Dead! Impossible! We can't have a dead person in The Haliburton. I knew hosting a dog show was a bad idea."

One of the guards cleared his throat and nodded his head indicating those of us who were participating in the show.

The hotel manager took the hint and quickly tried to backtrack. "I mean it was a bad idea to not have more security. If you will excuse me, I will go call the police."

He spoke to his guards. "Calvin. Todd. Stay here."

He walked away, muttering about containing the crisis and hotel reputation.

Matt pointed to Hoffman. "Shouldn't we turn him over?"

Bruce and Calvin spoke in unison. "No!"

Calvin explained, "Police procedure requires that the body not be moved."

Bruce seemed surprised by Calvin's statement. "We can't disturb the evidence."

Bruce turned to Calvin and extended his hand. "Bruce Brantford. Private detective."

Calvin shook his hand. "Calvin Wainwright. Retired Clark County sheriff's deputy."

Calvin was in his mid-to-late fifties with salt and pepper hair and an athletic build. The mocha-skinned guard stood over six feet tall. "This is Todd Givens. He currently is a sheriff's deputy."

Givens, who had been part of the dog chase, and Bruce shook hands.

Givens was just shy of six feet. His bright red hair and green eyes made me think he was Irish.

He smiled easily. "I moonlight as a guard for the extra money."

Bruce introduced the rest of us, then he, Calvin, and Givens started discussing the situation.

I checked on Paw. He continued to huddle on one side of the mastiff while the Chihuahua curled on the other. The mastiff lay with his head on his paws staring forlornly at his deceased master.

Matt had tried to get Lila away from the mastiff, but she wouldn't budge. He stood close to the dogs trying to guard her.

I motioned for Shelbee and Jac to step with me to the side. "I want to look around. See if I can find any clues."

Jac said, "I'll distract the guards."

Shelbee whispered as she walked past me, "I'll get Matt back from the body."

"Thanks."

I moved close to the dogs and examined the scene. I took a thorough look at the body. I knew better than to touch anything. I was careful where I placed my feet as well. The police would be collecting kibble from the floor as evidence.

Other than the matted blood in Hoffman's hair and the choker collar, the rest of his body was buried under kibble so I couldn't tell if he had further injuries. The red choker collar was cinched tight around his neck. I wasn't sure if it was the cause of his death or if it was the head wound. The head wound had matted the blood in his hair, but there wasn't a lot of blood nor could I see a deep wound or gash.

I had seen the same red choker dog collar and leash on Hoffman's dresser when I searched his room. Could it be the same one?

I hated the use of choker collars and winced to think of one being used to kill a person.

To the right of the body a small shovel lay on a pile of kibble. The shovel was about three feet in length with a wooden handle. A small amount of blood stained the metal head of the shovel. Most likely it was the object to cause Hoffman's head trauma. I saw no blood on the kibble or the bags.

Paw had stood up and walked to my side.

I absently patted his head while I continued to observe the scene. I scanned the piles of dog food but saw nothing else out of place.

Turning, I considered the piles of boxes lying on the floor behind me. They blocked the left most aisle that connected this vending area with the side and main doors where we had entered. The boxes appeared to have been part of a display for pizza-flavored dog treats and were replicas of takeout pizza boxes like one would get from a pizza restaurant. They had been stacked up as part of a display to advertise the dog treats.

I looked to my right at the closed side door at the end of the hall. I wondered if it was locked.

Paw woofed, distracting me. He jumped up onto the pile of dog food to one side of Hoffman's body. Kibble cascaded down as his heavier weight displaced it, causing him to sink partway into the kibble.

Calvin reacted immediately. "Hey! Get that dog out of there. He's disturbing evidence."

I groaned. Reaching Paw meant stepping into the kibble and further disturbing evidence.

I knew Paw wouldn't listen to me when I called him. He was intently sniffing the pile of kibble.

"Paw! Come here."

He ignored me and began to dig.

Calvin growled. "I said, stop the dog!"

I glanced up to see the two guards plus Bruce running toward me. Jac trailed behind. Shelbee had gotten Matt as far away as the pet portraitist's stand. She and Matt were now rushing over as well.

I tried to reach Paw's leash and almost toppled into the kibble pile.

Paw woofed again.

Lila jumped up and raced back and forth trying to block everyone's approach. She was a tiny thing, but she had the heart of a lion. She weaved in and out of legs, managing to trip Calvin, who fell forward onto his knees.

His partner, Todd, just managed to stop before falling over Calvin.

The mastiff had raised his head and growled low in

his throat.

Paw continued frantically digging.

Suddenly he stopped and stared at me then at the hole he dug and back to me.

Shelbee spoke near my shoulder. "I think he found something." She had quietly walked closer without alarming the mastiff.

Lila stopped running back and forth and allowed Matt to pick her up.

The mastiff watched the other men carefully. He didn't seem inclined to let them near.

Shelbee was taller than me so I suggested she edge around the pile of kibble and see if she could see what was in the hole.

Jac came up to us.

The mastiff let her by without complaint, but when Bruce and the guards stepped closer, he gave another warning growl.

Jac asked Shelbee, "Why don't Clarissa and I hold your arms to steady you so you can lean in closer?" Jac offered.

"That might work."

The three of us worked together.

Shelbee got a brief glimpse into the hole before starting to overbalance.

Jac and I righted her before she could fall face first in the kibble.

Paw had happily climbed down from the kibble pile now that he had gotten our attention.

Shelbee stepped out of the kibble. "I think it's a dog

brush. I saw black bristles, but the kibble is covering most of it."

She jerked her head at the body. "I wonder if it's connected."

Jac scanned the kibble for more clues. "Do you think the murderer could have dropped it?"

Calvin walked up to us. "I think you should get away from the body. And find someone to control these dogs."

I grabbed Paw's leash and noticed Matt held Lila closer to him.

Bruce asked, "What are we going to do about the mastiff?"

Todd hesitated to approach the mastiff. "I can call animal control."

Paw tensed at this remark.

I did too. The poor dog had just lost his master. He may not have been the most agreeable of pets, but he didn't need to go to animal control.

The dogs' ears perked up.

Faint hammering could be heard further in the hall.

Matt's Chihuahua jumped out of his arms and ran toward the sound, barking.

Paw pulled me after him.

I had to run at top speed to keep up. Matt was right behind me as was Bruce. I had no time to look back to see if anyone else followed.

Lila led us to a closed door on the back wall. Someone pounded on the closed door, begging, "Help me! Let me out!"

A frantic yipping sounded inside as well.

I reached forward to try the door handle. It was locked.

I called through the door. "Hold on. We'll get you out."

A woman's voice called back, on a sob. "Please hurry."

The voice was familiar, but I couldn't place to whom it belonged.

Paw was standing up, scratching at the door. Lila was sniffing at the crack at the bottom of the door. Both dogs were barking excitedly and answering barks could be heard behind the door.

I turned to Bruce. "We need a key."

Calvin joined us. "The manager has the key."

Behind us, footsteps approached.

Jac and the manager joined our group.

Jac whispered to me, "Shelbee is staying with the mastiff."

I nodded. If anyone could keep the mastiff calm, it would be Shelbee. She had an amazing way with animals.

The manager demanded, "What's happening here? Can't you calm these dogs."

Calvin explained, "We heard cries and traced it to this closet. A woman is locked inside."

The manager reached for the door knob. "Impossible!"

I grasped Paw's leash and pulled him back from the door.

Matt picked up Lila and cuddled her.

He grasped the knob, but it didn't turn. He bent his head, scanning the floor then pointed to a wooden block.

He addressed Calvin. "Why isn't the block in place?"

"I don't know, sir."

Bruce nudged the block with his foot. "Is this to keep the door from closing?"

The manager rolled his eyes. "Of course."

Jac frowned. "Why do you need a block to keep the door open?"

From the other side, the woman began pounding on the door. "Get me out. Now!"

The manager pulled out his keyring and selected a key. He inserted it, and the door clicked open.

Paw tensed, preparing to rush in, but I grabbed and held tight to his leash.

I recognized the woman standing in the doorway holding a Pomeranian. It was Dorothy Hawkins.

She looked frightened with wide eyes, rumpled clothes, and streaked makeup. She held the small dog cuddled tightly to her chest.

Behind her, I noticed rolls of paper towels and bottles of liquid on shelves. The room must be a supply closet.

Paw began to growl, and the Chihuahua joined in. The Pomeranian looked down at Paw and growled in return. I'd never known Paw to take an instant dislike to another dog except for our old neighbor's Pomeranian. Perhaps Paw thought this was the same dog. Both the Pomeranian and Dorothy appeared to be shaking slightly.

I grasped Paw's collar with my other hand. I didn't want Paw to scare the Pomeranian.

The night manager said to Dorothy, "My dear lady. Please accept my deepest apologies for your mishap."

Dorothy glared at the manager. "Mishap? Mishap! I was pushed into that closet. Someone attacked me!"

Paw growled low in his throat while the other dogs began to bark.

I tugged his collar. "Hush!"

He ignored me.

Dorothy was sobbing. "My poor Bitsy and I could have been killed. Who knows how long we could have been stuck in that closet?"

The manager continued to try soothing her. "I'm sure it was most upsetting."

He shot a warning glare at Paw's growling.

Bruce nudged me. "I think Paw needs to get out of here so everyone can calm down."

I gave him a dirty look.

Paw was just as upset as everyone else.

Jac put a hand on my back. Leaning in, she whispered, "Why not let me take Paw and see if we can help Shelbee to get the mastiff somewhere away from the body. The police are arriving, and I overheard them mentioning animal control."

I grimaced. No way did I want animal control taking charge of the mastiff. He was grief-stricken and likely to bite someone in his agitation. I may not have felt comfortable with him when he was protecting Hoffman, but he needed good care. The kind of care Shelbee could give. Paw had seemed to calm the mastiff earlier, so it was worth a try.

Jac had known just what to say to get me to let her take Paw away.

I pulled on Paw's collar, guiding him away from Dorothy.

He obeyed reluctantly.

I stopped and stared into his eyes. "Go with Jac. Help her and Shelbee with the mastiff."

He looked at me mulishly. He didn't want to leave me.

I caressed his ears. "I'll be okay."

He looked back at Dorothy and the night manager who were still talking. Then he looked at me. He gave my face a slurp and allowed Jac to walk him away.

I turned and returned to the group around Dorothy.

Dorothy was saying, "Someone pushed me. Don't you dare accuse me of imagining things!"

The manager's attempts to calm her were not going well. It didn't help that he was trying to cover his butt for any lawsuits against the hotel.

Matt was watching quietly.

Both the Chihuahua and the Pomeranian had stopped barking and were sitting quietly in their owners' arms.

Bruce was behind Dorothy with Calvin examining the closet door's knob and lock.

I stepped over to them and looked into the closet then stepped inside.

It was a typical cleaning closet with limited room to

stand due to the various cleaning equipment piled along the walls. There was a cleaning cart loaded with bottles and brushes, a mop bucket and mops, plus brooms and other cleaning equipment. One side had shelves loaded with paper towels and cleaning bottles of liquid. Dorothy was a tall woman, well-built woman, bigger than my height at five-foot-two inches. I would have felt cramped in here. Dorothy wouldn't have been able to maneuver in such a small space. No wonder she was frantic to get out. It was a wonder she hadn't hit her head or been injured when she was pushed into the closet. I realized that none of us had asked her if she was injured.

I stepped out of the closet past Bruce and Calvin. I overheard Calvin say to Bruce that the lock and knob showed no signs of tampering.

The night clerk had arrived and was speaking with the hotel manager. Dorothy was continuing to argue with the manager as well. Matt was nowhere in sight.

The clerk said, "Sir, the police are here. What do you want to do?"

The manager hesitated, looking over at Dorothy. He was clearly debating what to do with her.

I stepped up and put an arm around Dorothy. "I'll stay with Dorothy."

This time he glanced at me with gratitude. "Don't go far."

He turned and strode back toward the crime scene with everyone but Dorothy and I following him.

I looked up at Dorothy. "Why don't we go somewhere

quiet and sit for a while?"

Sniffling, she said, "I could use a nice cup of tea. I have the supplies in my stall. It's right over there."

She pointed up a nearby aisle.

"Good idea."

Together we walked a short distance up the aisle to her stall.

I took the time to look at her carefully.

Her face had regained some of its color from her argument with the manager. Her clothes were still disheveled, and her hair stood on end.

Bitsy was quiet. Her fur lay flat, and her pink bow sat askew on her head.

"Are you hurt, Dorothy? Did you hit your head when the person pushed you into the closet?"

"No dear. My nerves are all a flutter, but I'm not physically hurt. I managed to catch my balance before I reached the shelves. My poor little Bitsy is so upset that she is shaking." She hugged the dog to her protectively.

I urged Dorothy to sit when we reached her stall.

She pointed to the tea making supplies. She had an electric kettle that I poured bottled water in to make the tea. While the water heated, I grabbed a bowl for Bitsy and added fresh bottled water.

She happily jumped down to drink.

I set out two cups, sugar, and a small carton of milk

kept in a portable cooler. Dorothy had a well-stocked stall. She sat in silence while I finished making the tea.

Trembling, she took the cup of tea I handed her. "Thank you. You are kind to comfort Bitsy and me."

"I'm happy to help. It must have been terribly frightening, stuck in that closet."

"Yes. It was. It was so small and full of stuff I couldn't move." She shuddered. "I was so scared that she would come back and hurt me."

"She!"

"Yes. I'm sure it was a woman."

I breathed on my tea to cool it. "How can you be sure?"

"I smelled perfume just before she shoved me into the closet."

"Could it have been a man's cologne?"

"No, it was a woman's perfume. A floral scent."

I suppose I looked dubious because she continued to explain. "I used to work at a perfume sales counter before marrying my husband – God rest his soul. You develop a sensitive nose when working around so much perfume. I would know that fragrance anywhere."

I took a sip of tea. "I guess I just assumed it was a man who pushed you. Dorothy, could you tell me what happened, starting from the beginning? Maybe we can get a better idea of who might have done this to you. That is if you feel up to it."

"I do feel calmer. A good cup of tea helps everything."

Bitsy jumped up on her lap.

She cooed to the Pomeranian "And my little sweetheart does too." Clearly, she loved her dog, and Bitsy was wiggling in delight at the attention.

Dorothy continued. "I went to the closet to get a broom to sweep my stall. I know the hotel has the staff to do that, but I am a bit of a neat freak. Besides, Bitsy couldn't seem to settle down. Too excited by the show, I guess. I thought if we stayed in the hall a while she would calm down. Almost everyone had left or were leaving, and things were nice and quiet.

"I took Bitsy with me because she fussed so when I started to walk away. I had her in my arms and had just opened the door to the closet when Bitsy started to growl.

"Before I could turn around someone put a hand on my shoulders and shoved. I could smell a whiff of the floral perfume and was about to turn around and yell at her when the door slammed shut.

"It was totally dark in there. I felt for the door and tried the knob, but it wouldn't turn. I pounded on the door and yelled for help for the longest time, but no one came until your group showed up."

I gasped. "That's terrible. I'm surprised we didn't hear you when we first came into the hall."

Dorothy flushed. "After a while, I gave up and sat on the floor cuddling Bitsy. I may have fallen into a doze. I was so exhausted from banging on the door and yelling."

"Surely one of the few remaining people in the hall would have heard something or saw someone."

Dorothy's voice hardened. "If they did, they didn't help me."

"I'm sure it wasn't intentional. Maybe they were too far away."

Dorothy nodded. "Could be."

"Dorothy. There is something I have to ask you. Did you hear any noises or raised voices while you were in the closet?"

"I don't think so. I did think I heard a bump like something falling, but when I started pounding on the door, no one came."

"Maybe that's a good thing."

She looked at me in surprise.

"I have to tell you why we are all in the hall. Gerald Hoffman is dead. He was murdered."

Dorothy gasped. "How?"

I recounted everything that happened from the chase of the dogs to finding the body.

"I can't believe it. Who would do such a thing?" She gasped. "Do you think the person who locked me in the closet was the murderer?"

I hesitated, afraid to worry her further. "It could be."

Her voice shook as it raised in volume. "Oh dear, oh dear, oh dear!"

I refreshed her tea and urged her to drink.

Bitsy was pawing her face, trying to comfort her.

Dorothy's tears dripped down her cheeks. "Maybe I'm next."

"Dorothy. Try not to worry. Most likely, it wasn't the

killer. And even if it was, it appears whoever pushed you meant you no harm. I think they just wanted to get you out of the way."

Her tears slowed.

"Dorothy –"

I was interrupted by a commanding female voice. "Which one of you is Clarissa Brantford?"

I turned to see a tall, coffee-skinned woman wearing a conservative black-and-gray striped dress-suit standing at the entrance to Dorothy's stall.

I stood. "I am."

She observed me a moment. "I'm Detective Gibbons. I need to speak with you."

She glanced at Dorothy. "Who are you, ma'am?"

"Dorothy Hawkins."

"You're the woman who was locked in the closet?"

"Yes. Me and Bitsy."

The detective looked puzzled. "Who is Bitsy?

I pointed to the Pomeranian in Dorothy's lap.

The detective rolled her eyes. Dorothy gave her a cold look.

The detective gestured to me. "Mrs. Brantford, I need you to come with me."

She gestured to the uniformed officer standing behind her. "Mrs. Hawkins, please go with Officer Randall and give him your statement."

I squeezed Dorothy's shoulder in comfort as I walked past her. "I'll check on you later."

She smiled up at me.

CHAPTER 10

I follow Detective Gibbons down the aisle and over several more to a booth the police had commandeered for their command center.

The detective walked quickly with determined steps.

I had to double time it to keep up.

The command center was in a ten-by-ten-foot booth. It contained a long table and six folding chairs, three along each side of the table's length.

Detective Gibbons pointed to a chair, indicating I should sit. She rounded the table to sit opposite me. "Mrs. Brantford. I understand that you were one of the people to discover the body. Is that correct?"

"Yes."

She opened a notebook and picked up a pen. "Could you please describe what you saw?"

I gathered my thoughts. "The lights were off in the hall when we entered. The main doors were locked, but the side door my friends and I entered through was unlocked."

The detective asked, "Were both doors closed?"

"Yes."

She waved me to continue.

I began, "The dogs ran ahead into the dark."

"Dogs?"

"Yes. Hoffman's mastiff was locked in their hotel room. The dog was barking to get out, and someone called the night manager to investigate."

Detective Gibbons held up her pen. "Who called the night manager?"

"Matt Monroe. He's the owner of the Chihuahua who found the body."

"Wait!" Gibbons sat back. "I thought you found the body."

I nodded. "A bunch of us found the body."

Gibbons frowned. "Go back to where the mastiff was locked in Mr. Hoffman's room and continue from there, please."

I folded my hands in my lap. "The night manager knocked on Hoffman's door, trying to get Hoffman's attention, but no one answered. He had the guard who was with him open the door.

"The mastiff rushed out, and our dogs followed. You see, my friends and I and Matt Monroe had stepped out into the hallway at the sound of the dog's distress. I believe there were several other witnesses who were in the hall as well.

"The dogs ran to the elevator, got in, and my dog, Paw, pushed one of the buttons, closing the doors."

Gibbons raised an eyebrow but nodded for me to continue.

"My...husband, the manager, guard, and Mr. Monroe took the stairwell down to catch the dogs. My friends, Shelbee and Jac, and I followed. There was a chase in the lobby, and then the mastiff ran down the hall and stopped at the main doors of the event room. He howled and scratched along with our dogs, who had followed.

"As I said, my friends and I went in the side door, but the men came in the main door because the manager had the key. They were the ones who turned on the lights.

"We met up and heard the mastiff howling further in the room, but couldn't see him for the stalls.

"We walked down the aisles, but my friends and I had to move over to another aisle because a pile of boxes blocked the end of the aisle."

Gibbons asked, "Was that unusual?"

I shook my head. "Yes. It appeared as though a display had been knocked over into the aisle."

She motioned for me to continue.

"We moved into the next aisle, and when we reached the end, we saw the dogs standing around a pile of kibble in front of a vending stall.

"A man was sprawled face down in the kibble.

"We approached, and my husband checked for a pulse, but the man was dead. The back of his head had matted blood, and a red choker dog collar encircled his neck, cinched tight."

Gibbons's expression remained blank. "Did you touch anything at the scene?"

I sighed. "Yes."

She looked up from her notebook, wearing a frown. "What did you touch?"

"I didn't touch anything, but my dog jumped up on the kibble pile and began to dig. Paw uncovered what we think is a brush."

She glowered. "You think?"

I shrugged. "It was half-covered in kibble."

Gibbons called to an officer. "Go see if one of the techs found anything in the kibble. If so, bring the bagged evidence to me right away."

The officer nodded and left.

Gibbons turned back to her notebook. "Did you know the victim?"

"Not really. I only met him today after entering the dog show."

Detective Gibbons looked up at me from her note taking. "You're entered in the show?"

"Yes."

She continued to stare at me.

Feeling I should explain, I said, "My husband and I entered our Saint Bernard in the competition."

She still looked incredulous. "I see," she said, but her tone said that she thought I was crazy to enter a dog show. "What can you tell me about the victim? Was he in the dog show, too?"

I knew I had to answer carefully. I had to talk to Bruce to find out how much he wanted the police to know of his investigation. I was already lying about my name. "Hoffman was in the dog show with his mastiff. They lost their breed competition today, or rather yesterday since it is after midnight."

Gibbons wrote in her book. "How did he get along with the others? Did you talk with him?"

"I spoke with him once, trying to be friendly. He didn't get along with others too well. He put in a complaint against the judge who was judging his breed competition. Claimed the judge was not impartial, I believe."

"Can you name anyone besides the judge who had a disagreement with Mr. Hoffman?"

I sighed. "He had a verbal confrontation with Matt Monroe. Matt thought Hoffman was wrong to complain about the judge, but I can't see that as the reason for his death."

Gibbons looked skeptical. "Anyone else?"

"Not that I can think of."

She continued to stare at me. This time I kept my mouth shut.

"Give me the names of your friends and husband."

"Shelbee Van Vight. Jacqueline Weldon. And my husband, Bruce Brantford."

She was staring at her notes and had just opened her

mouth when the officer returned with the evidence bag. "Detective, here's what they found. They requested you join them at the scene as soon as possible. They found something."

Gibbons nodded to him, then pushed the bag toward me. "Does this look like what you found?"

I observed the contents of the bag. A black brush with black bristles was just visible through the kibble embedded in its bristles and coating the brush's sides. I thought I saw a bit of gold color on a corner of the brush, but couldn't be sure.

I smiled weakly. "I guess. My friend, Shelbee, was the one who peeked into the hole Paw dug."

Gibbons raised her brows. "Paw?"

"That's my dog's name."

She nodded and stood up. "That will be all right now, Mrs. Brantford. You will be required to stay here at the show until told otherwise. We may have more questions for you."

She stepped to the entrance of the booth then turned around and looked at me. "One last question: did your dog win?"

"No. He didn't win his breed."

She nodded, picked up the evidence bag, and walked away.

I needed to find Bruce to coordinate our stories. Hopefully, I could talk to him before he spoke with Gibbons. I assumed Bruce was at the crime scene, so I headed that way. I could see lots of police personnel around the vending booths. The police had cordoned off the crime scene and stationed officers at the perimeter to keep the rest of us out. A small crowd of people was spread out along the tape trying to get a view of what was happening. I joined them, searching for Bruce.

I was scanning the scene when a voice next to me said, "Bad business isn't it?"

I turned and saw Jed Gray standing next to me.

"Yes, it is," I said.

I realized that I hadn't seen him all day and had completely forgotten about him.

Jed sighed. "It is hard to believe one of us was murdered."

I looked at him sharply. *How did he know someone was killed, let alone murdered?*

He saw my look and smiled sadly. "I met your friends Shelbee and Jac on the stairs and asked about Samuel."

I stared blankly.

He smiled again. "Samuel is ..." He paused, frowning. "... was Hoffman's mastiff. I wondered why he ran off."

"You're on the same floor as us?"

"Yes. I heard the noise the dogs made and saw you rush off after them. I wheedled the information out of Shelbee."

"How do you know Shelbee? The shows?"

He smiled. "I think almost everyone knows Shelbee. She has been a huge help to a lot of our dogs and us."

I was surprised Shelbee had told Jed about the body and vowed to ask her when I saw her. Not that the body would have been a secret for long.

Jed shook his head. "Hoffman could be difficult to get along with at the shows, but murder? It doesn't seem possible."

"Is there anyone, in particular, he didn't get along with?"

"I really can't think of anyone."

I doubted that. Hoffman didn't seem to get along with anyone from what I observed. "Did you ever have a disagreement with him?"

He looked at me sharply. "Not really."

He seemed too evasive, but I let it go.

I was curious why I hadn't seen him earlier in the day? "How did your dog do in his competitions?"

"Competition. Tucker didn't make it through his breed. He's getting older, like me, and doesn't show as well. Honestly, I come more to see old friends than to expect to win any awards."

"Did you have time to visit old friends?"

"Yes. I had time."

I was tempted to ask why I hadn't seen him or where he had been at the time of the murder. I realized I didn't know when the murder had taken place, but I had a window of time when I thought it had happened. The show had been over around five o'clock, and the dogs had begun the chase at around eight o'clock, so that left a three-hour window of time.

I decided that right now I needed to find Bruce rather than continue questioning Jed. I doubted he would give me any satisfactory answers, anyway.

I excused myself and continued to search for Bruce.

I walked through the hall around the rest of the crime tape but couldn't find Bruce. He must have left the hall. I decided to check in the lobby before going up to our room. Perhaps he was talking to one of the guards or the hotel manager.

I left the hall through the main entrance passing a uniformed officer who was stationed there to keep people out. A small group of people was arguing with the guard to get inside. I recognized several show participants and one well-known TV reporter.

The hallway leading to the lobby had a steady stream of police going back and forth. The formerly quiet lobby was a beehive of activity when I entered. Police rushed around doing who knows what, while show participants lingered out of curiosity and reporters asked questions of anyone who would listen to them.

Nowhere did I see Bruce. I spotted the hotel clerk who had helped in the dog chase. He was standing to the side of the desk while the hotel manager fielded questions from his position behind the desk.

I pushed through people to get to the clerk's side.

His wide grin reassured me that he recognized me.

"Have you seen my husband, Mr. Brantford?"

"He was in the lobby with the manager and guards a little while ago, but then he left, and I don't know where he went."

"Thank you."

⁓

I decided to go upstairs and look for him. There was no way that I was going to have a chance to ask the hotel manager any questions.

I took the elevator up to my floor. I was the only one on it. All the action was centered downstairs. The elevator doors opened. Everything was quiet here. I reached my door and knocked, hoping Shelbee and Jac were here. In a rush to chase the dogs, I had forgotten my room key.

Bruce opened the door. He smiled and pulled me into the room.

Shelbee and Jac sat on the bed with Paw and the mastiff.

Both dogs' tongues lolled out of their mouths as my friends massaged them. Jac was massaging Paw while Shelbee was massaging Samuel.

The mastiff sighed contentedly, more docile than I had seen him previously.

Shelbee was the first to speak. "How's Dorothy?"

"She was calmer when I left her. I hope she stayed that way when questioned."

Jac was massaging Paw's feet. "The police questioned Dorothy?"

I nodded. "Yes. Me too."

Bruce cursed. "I was hoping to talk with you before they questioned us. What did they ask you?"

I recounted my interview with Gibbons. "The usual. I explained how I came to be in the events hall and what I saw. I told her about Paw digging in the hole. She sent an officer to get the evidence. Weren't you questioned?"

"No. The officers took our names and requested we stay in our room. I expect they'll be here soon. The evidence – Did you see it?"

"Briefly. It was a brush encrusted with kibble, and I thought I saw a gold edge, but otherwise it was black with black bristles like Shelbee described. We're going to run into problems with lying about our names, aren't we?"

"Maybe. A false name probably wouldn't be too much of a concern unless the police think we used them while planning to commit a crime."

Jac stopped massaging Paw. "Like murder?"

Bruce grunted. "Yeah."

I asked him, "Do you know Detective Gibbons?"

"I know of her, but I've never met her. Her second-in-command is Sergeant Bull. I have worked with him, and we got along well. Perhaps that can help us out. The best thing is for me to explain why I am here and that you are working for me. That way it will look less suspicious to the detective."

"She'll wonder why I didn't tell her that in the first place."

"Let her wonder. If she asks, just tell her I instructed you to keep everything confidential, including your identity."

Shelbee finished the mastiff's massage. "Did Dorothy tell you what happened to her?"

Jac was now caressing Paw's ears.

He wore a big goofy smile on his face.

I related everything that Dorothy had told me. "She is sure a woman pushed her into that closet. She claims she smelled perfume."

Jac stopped massaging Paw's ears. "Perfume? Won't it be hard to find the person who wore it?"

"Dorothy swears she will know the scent again."

Jac pointed out. "There could be hundreds of people who wear that same perfume."

Shelbee began brushing Samuel. "True. The question is, do they have a reason to have pushed Dorothy into the closet?"

Bruce wondered. "Why push her into it in the first place?"

I suggested. "The killer wanted her out of the way."

"Maybe," Bruce said. "But why not just kill Dorothy while killing Hoffman?"

Jac thought about it. "Maybe the killer hadn't planned on killing Hoffman. He, or she, pushed Dorothy into the closet planning to confront Hoffman and things got out of control. Perhaps, Hoffman was killed in a fit of rage."

Shelbee said. "I find it odd that Dorothy didn't hear the fight or killing."

I sat on the settee. "I do too. She did hear some noise, but perhaps the closet dampens sound. That would be something we can test out."

"Why would Dorothy lie, though?"

"She could be scared. She was frightened in that closet, and when I mentioned Hoffman's death, she was afraid she could have been killed. Maybe she feels safer not admitting to hearing anything."

Bruce agreed. "She may be afraid the killer will come after her if she admits to knowing anything. Of course, she has already admitted to smelling perfume."

I said, "But that was before she knew of the murder. She just thought someone had played a cruel trick on her when she mentioned the perfume."

Jac wondered, "Could it have been someone helping the murderer?"

Bruce stood with his hands on his hips. "Anything is possible. Let's review what we saw at the crime scene. Perhaps one of us picked up a clue that the rest didn't."

We took turns describing what we saw, interrupting each other if we noticed something different. With minor differences, we came to a working model of what we saw and some basic conclusions.

I said, "It looked like a struggle with the boxes over-turned and the bags of kibble toppled over and kibble scattered everywhere. But we don't know if the blow to the head from the shovel or the dog collar around Hoffman's neck was the cause of death."

Jac asked, "How can we find out?"

Bruce smiled. "Leave that to me. I have friends in the Dockers Police Department who can tell me what the coroner determines is the cause of death. Plus, I can find out the time of death."

I said, "From my calculation, he was killed sometime between five and eight pm."

Jac gaped at me. "How did you figure that?"

"We left the hall around five o'clock to come up here to eat. There were plenty of people in the hall when we left. I doubt he was killed with so many people still around. The Mastiff was howling and started the chase at around eight o'clock. I remember looking at my watch. Sometime in between those times has to be the time of death."

Bruce agreed.

Jac stood up. "What is next?"

I stood up and searched my suitcase for pen and paper. "We need to make a list of suspects and check out their alibis. The three of us can do that while Bruce finds out the cause of death."

"Who are our suspects? Seems to me our suspect is the dead one."

Shelbee raised her head. "Could we have two murderers on the loose? The one who killed Connors and the one who murdered Hoffman?"

Jac added, "Or did someone kill Hoffman as revenge for Connors's murder?"

I blew out a breath. "I don't know. I think both murders are connected to the dog shows, so our best bet is to consider anyone connected to the show."

Bruce began pacing. "Hoffman made a lot of enemies."

"So did Connors from the sound of it. Which reminds me of something Hoffman said when I questioned him. He said that he would have suspected Dorothy's husband, Fred, of killing Connors if he hadn't already been dead."

"We need to find out more about past grievances." Bruce looked at me. "Do you think Dorothy would tell you about her husband's relationship with Connors and Hoffman?"

"I think so," I said. "But we need to look at Matt and his girlfriend too. Colby had good reason to want Connors dead. Maybe she had a reason to kill Hoffman as well. One more thing, I want to question Jed Gray."

I told them of my recent encounter with him.

Shelbee asked, "Judge Gray?"

"I didn't know he was a judge. I thought he was just a competitor in the dog shows."

"He isn't a dog show judge. He's a retired circuit court judge. Why do you want to question him?"

I shrugged. "Because I didn't see him all day until after the murder and he was evasive when I asked him some questions."

Bruce stopped pacing. "Judge Gray is well-known and

well-respected for his judicial work. I highly doubt he committed murder."

Shelbee nodded. "Plus, he is a real sweetheart."

Jac disagreed. "I think Clarissa is right, though. It is suspicious how he wasn't around and then turns up at the murder scene."

Shelbee shrugged. "I can't see him as a murderer. And Jac and I did tell him about it when we came upstairs. I figured it was okay since he used to be a judge."

A knock sounded at the door.

Both dogs jumped off the bed and rushed to the door, barking.

CHAPTER 11

J hurried over and grabbed Paw's collar while Shelbee urged the mastiff back from the door.

Bruce opened the door to Detective Gibbons who stood there flanked by two uniformed officers.

She looked at the two dogs cautiously. "Bruce Brantford?"

"Yes."

"I need to question you regarding the death of Mr. Gerald Hoffman."

She looked at my friends. "Are you Shelbee Van Vight and Jacqueline Weldon?"

"I am Shelbee."

"I'm Jac."

Detective Gibbons frowned. "Are these two of the dogs who compromised the crime scene?"

I bristled at her tone. "We didn't know we were stumbling onto a crime scene when we went into the hall."

"But you didn't pull them away immediately. In fact, as you confessed, one of them dug into the dog food at the scene, possibly compromising it."

"At least he found some evidence."

Detective Gibbons nostrils flared as she gave me a cold look.

Bruce stepped in before we had a confrontation, though. "It is done, detective. How can we help you to solve this murder?"

"By letting us do our job and cooperating with us," she shot back at him. Taking a deep breath, she regained her composure. "Mr. Brantford, will you come with me and answer my questions? Officers Garrett and Watkins will take Ms. Van Vight and Ms. Weldon's statements."

She looked at me. "Keep the dogs here and out of trouble. We may need to take DNA or print samples from them."

I dipped my head in acknowledgment, even though I was fuming.

She looked at the dogs as if they were a nuisance.

Bruce followed the detective out of the room.

With a squeeze to each of my arms, Shelbee and Jac allowed the other officers to escort them away for questioning.

The mastiff whined at Shelbee's departure.

I patted his head, and Paw leaned against him. The poor dog had had a terrible night.

As I shut the room door, I noticed another uniformed officer knocking on Matt's door. I wondered if Lila would face the same evidence gathering as Paw and Samuel.

I closed the door and turned to the dogs. Both looked expectantly at me.

I glanced at my watch, nearly two a.m. The late hour explained why I was exhausted. Now that the adrenaline rush of everything that happened was wearing off, my eyes were drooping. Who knew how long everyone's questioning would take?

"What say we lay down and try to rest," I said to the dogs. They wagged their tails in agreement and followed me to the bed.

Paw immediately jumped up on the bed as I lay down. With a little coaxing, the mastiff joined us.

I felt nearly smothered with two big dogs by me, but comforted as well. A murderer was on the loose. I didn't think I was a target, but it was reassuring to have two capable dogs there with me.

I tried to sleep, but though my tired body wanted to rest, my mind continued to race.

Who could have killed Hoffman? He could be abrasive and harsh, but is that why someone killed him?

I thought of everyone he had confronted the previous day. The judge he had accused of misconduct and Matt Monroe were the two most obvious suspects. Had Hoffman fought with others?

I would have to find out. I hadn't met the judge, but he should be easy to find to question. But would he kill over something like Hoffman's complaint?

That's when I remembered the complaint against Hoffman. Who had complained and what was the cause of the complaint? Was Hoffman killed over that dispute?

Of course, it was possible that his death came from a past dispute. I wondered if Hoffman's death was connected to Connors. How could the two be connected?

Matt was one connection. Connors had besmirched his girlfriend's name. Had Hoffman complained about her as well? Colby was here at the show too. Dorothy had said she smelled perfume. Did Colby wear perfume and the same kind? Could she have sought revenge on both men and spared Dorothy?

I had too many questions and no answers. My mind was still restless, but I must have fallen asleep anyway for I remembered dreaming of being locked in a closet.

Dorothy was offering me tea, saying it solved any problem while Paw scratched at the closet door. Colby sat in a chair at a table feeding Lila little biscuits while Matt crawled on the floor like a dog. Tuck sat next to Lila. Beside them, Judge Gray was sipping tea. On the other side of the closet door, the mastiff was barking and knocking. Paw turned to me. "Clarissa. Open the door." More barking.

I woke enough to realize that the dogs really were barking. I could hear Bruce's voice from the other side of the hotel door as he knocked insistently. I struggled out of bed, having entangled myself in the sheets and the clothes I had worn to bed instead of removing them. My one shoe-clad foot twisted in the sheet and I landed on the floor with a plop.

"Clarissa! Are you okay?" Bruce demanded, still knocking. The dogs continued to bark, running back and forth between me and the door.

I heard a muffled voice demand, "Hey! Keep it down. Some of us are trying to sleep." Followed by a muttered, "Stuck on a floor with dogs."

"Sorry," Bruce said.

I got to my feet, shushing the dogs, and unlocked the room door.

Bruce rushed in, took one look at my disheveled appearance, and gave me a big hug. It felt heavenly. "No Shelbee or Jac yet?"

"No. I fell asleep waiting for all of you to return."

"Sorry to wake you."

"It's all right. How did it go?"

"Gibbons wasn't happy about a private eye being here, but I think we're in the clear. At least, she doesn't act like she thinks we're the murderers. She warned me to stay out of her investigation, but I can't do that. We'll just have to be extra subtle."

"What did she ask you?"

"About the same as you. She noted down the information on Connors, but I got the impression she didn't think it was important to her case. I'm exhausted. Let me get some sleep, and we'll go over everything in the morning with Shelbee and Jac."

I agreed and gestured for Bruce to take the bed. He feebly protested but gratefully took it.

He was sound asleep the minute his head hit the

pillow.

Before long, Shelbee and Jac returned, tapping lightly on the door. I immediately opened with a finger to my lips, motioning to be quiet. I whispered, "Let's get some sleep and discuss things in the morning," which was only a few hours away.

We found extra blankets and pillows in the closet and bedded down on the floor. The dogs happily joined us.

I changed into pajamas, and so did Shelbee. Jac slept in her clothes since she hadn't originally planned to stay at the hotel. She did call her dad so he wouldn't worry what happened to her.

Morning came too soon. I woke to the smell of fresh coffee. Jac was helping the room service attendant unload his cart. I could hear Bruce snoring on the bed above me. Glancing to my left, I saw Shelbee stretching into a yoga pose. The room service attendant goggled at her. Jac smirked at me and directed him back out of the room. I sat up, dislodging Paw's front legs from my stomach. He opened his eyes and stared at me accusingly. I was disturbing his beauty sleep. I caressed his head then stood up. Samuel had followed Jac to the table. He sniffed the air, eager for food.

I went to the closet and selected two cans of dog food then prepared the bowls of food and fresh water. Paw jumped up when he heard the can opener. Both dogs eagerly ate their food but continued to stare at our food on the table.

I poured two cups of coffee and took one over to hold under Bruce's nose. He woke slowly, sniffing the coffee appreciatively. One eye opened, and he reached for the cup with a grunt. Leaving him to wake up I retrieved my cup and took a long swig. I normally didn't drink coffee, but after last night I needed the caffeine jolt to clear my head.

Shelbee finished her yoga routine and sat at the table. We filled plates with scrambled eggs, toast, bacon, and fresh fruit. Bruce joined us, filling his plate. We ate in silence for several minutes.

Jac was the first to speak. "I'm going to have to go home and change clothes, but I'll come back."

Bruce nodded. "Before you go, tell us about your questioning."

"Not much to tell. The officer wanted to know who I was and what I was doing here. Then he asked me to describe what I had seen and if I knew the victim. He wanted to know where I had been from five o'clock until we found the body."

Bruce said to me, "So your estimate of the time range for the death matches what the police are thinking."

"Sounds like it. I wish we could narrow the time down to a shorter range."

"We'll just have to work with what we have. What about you Shelbee?"

"The same questions. Where do we start today?"

Bruce thought a minute. "We need to question our suspects. I still think Connors's death and Hoffman's murder are connected." He nodded to Shelbee. "You spoke to Colby earlier. Go back and speak to her again. Find out where she was last night. I want to find out if she was the one to push Dorothy in the closet."

Bruce turned to me. "I need you to question Dorothy again. I want to know what the relationship was between her husband, Connors, and Hoffman. Maybe we can find a connection between the deaths."

"You think Dorothy's husband was murdered?"

"I'm considering the possibility."

The dogs started to whine. Shelbee looked up. "We better take them for a walk."

"All right." I looked at Bruce. "What are you going to do?"

"I'm going to talk to Sergeant Bull. He may be able to tell me what the police found out last night."

Jac finished her last bite. "Sergeant Bull? I don't recall meeting him last night."

"He wasn't here, but he is Detective Gibbons's second in command. He'll know everything she found out. The police will be back today to continue their investigation, and I bet Bull will be with them."

I asked Bruce, "Are we continuing undercover or should we reveal who we are?"

"For now, continue with our undercover story. If necessary, you can reveal why we are here to get the information we need."

Jac picked up her purse. "Bye, guys. I'll be back as soon as I can." She left our room.

Shelbee and I took the dogs down to the dog park. It was still early, but a few other dog show participants were walking their dogs. Both Samuel and Paw enjoyed sniffing out the park. We kept our dogs away from the others because we were uncertain how Samuel would react to them. He had become comfortable around Paw. The dogs took care of their morning routine, and I reached into my pants pocket for a treat for them. I had thrown on yesterday's clothes planning to change after walking the dogs. As I pulled out two treats, something small and white fell out of my pocket. I hurriedly grabbed it up from the grass as Paw was coming to investigate. I handed each dog a treat. Both happily crunched away, tails waving. I examined the object and discovered it was a white pill. My mind was blank for a minute.

Shelbee pointed at the pill. "I forgot about that in the excitement." She stared at my blank expression. "That's the pill you found in Hoffman's room."

"Now I remember. I suppose we should finish checking it out. You said Sal, the ex-veterinarian, would know what it is. Can you ask him today?"

"Sure. I better talk to Colby first then I'll find him."

"I wonder if the show will be canceled."

A woman walking past with her greyhound heard me. "Terrible what happened isn't it. The police are letting the show go on, though."

I thanked her for the information, and she walked on with her dog.

I asked Shelbee, "What is left of the show?"

"A few of the groups have to compete for the Best in Groups and then there is the Best in Show competition. After that, the show wraps up."

"That means we better make the most of today to find out who did it."

We returned to the hotel room. I showered and changed into fresh clothes.

Shelbee did the same. She always carried an overnight bag when she went to the shows in case she had to help an anxious dog owner. We left the room, leaving the dogs behind. Hopefully, they would settle down and sleep. Neither of us felt comfortable taking Samuel back into the hall and around all those people and dogs. He had calmed down and accepted us, but he had been through a trauma.

Shelbee didn't want to risk stressing him out yet.

Paw had willingly taken to his role as care dog. Together they should be fine for a few hours.

We parted ways at the hall entrance. Shelbee went to question Matt's girlfriend while I went in search of Dorothy.

I found her already at her stall, crooning to Bitsy as she groomed her.

"Hello, Dorothy. How are you?"

"Hello, dear. I'm feeling much better."

"Did you sleep well?"

"Not at first, so I took a sleeping pill. I kept worrying the murderer would come after me. Finally, I wedged a chair under my locked door. I hate taking pills, but I had to be at my best today for Bitsy's competition." She continued to brush Bitsy's hair in long strokes. Bitsy panted happily as the blue and white brush smoothed her hair. On the stand surrounding her lay combs, various sizes and colored brushes, and a multicolored array of bows.

"I slept fitfully, too, but I had both dogs in bed with me, so I felt secure. I couldn't stop thinking about Hoffman's death and who would want him dead."

"Hoffman was a difficult person to like. He had many arguments with others at the shows, but I can't believe it would lead to murder."

"Who did he argue with?"

Dorothy picked up a spray bottle and spritzed Bitsy's fur. "The mastiff judge for one, although Hoffman was wrong to complain. I've known Ken for several years, and he has always been fair."

I edged closer to see what she was spraying on Bitsy. Perhaps it was something I could use on Paw's fur. "I thought the judges would judge only one breed."

"No. They are knowledgeable in many breeds."

"So he has judged you in the past?"

Dorothy began to comb through Bitsy's fur. "Once. I've watched him judge others and like I said he has always been fair."

"Who else did Hoffman argue with?"

"Matt Monroe. At least that's what I heard. It doesn't surprise me, though."

I still couldn't see the label on the spray bottle. "Why is that?"

"Beatrice Stedman, Matt's aunt, had accused Gerald Hoffman of trying to sabotage her competition at a past show. Matt was there as well and backed up his aunt as did Colby, Matt's girlfriend," she said. "After that, Beatrice wouldn't speak to Gerald nor would he speak to her."

"How did Hoffman sabotage the competition?"

"A loose dog went running into the judging ring distracting Beatrice's Chihuahua, Lila, and causing her to lose points and her breed competition."

I sighed. I still couldn't see the label. "Just like what happened in the mastiff judging?"

"Yes." Dorothy set down the comb and picked up the spray bottle.

I read the spray bottle label – Van Coy Hair Conditioner. I knew Paw wouldn't let me use it on him. "What I don't understand is why Hoffman would want to ruin a Chihuahua competition. He breeds mastiffs."

Dorothy spritzed Bitsy again, creating a cloud of spray. "It has to do with Best in Show. Lila has won several times. If Hoffman hoped to win with his mastiff, he would need to eliminate some competition."

The little dog stayed contentedly standing as Dorothy began combing her.

I thought of Paw. He'd never stand still this long. "Didn't Lyon Connors accuse Hoffman of sabotage?"

"Yes. He did. But just like Mrs. Stedman's claim, nothing could be proved."

"From what I have heard, Connors was accused of sabotage as well."

Dorothy stiffened, causing the comb to pull Bitsy's hair and the little dog to yelp. Dorothy smoothed her hands over Bitsy's body. "I'm sorry, little girl."

Dorothy looked up at me. "That wasn't true. Lyon didn't sabotage anyone. He was a good competitor and successful, so people were quick to accuse him."

"I never met the man. You were friends with him?"

Dorothy picked up Bitsy and cuddled her. "He was closer to my husband, but we were all friends. I really can't see how Lyon's past has anything to do with Hoffman's death. Besides, poor Lyon is dead."

I sighed. "I didn't mean to upset you, Dorothy. I was just trying to understand past connections. I heard that Lyon had complained of negligence on Colby's part and wondered if there was a connection to Hoffman's and Matt's animosity toward each other."

"It's all right, dear. My husband's and Lyon's deaths are still too fresh. I loved my husband dearly and talking about Lyon brings all the memories back of the times we shared. I miss them both so much." She gave a sniff. "Lyon did accuse the girl of negligence. He adored his dogs, just like me, and took their care seriously. He never told me exactly what happened, but I know Lyon wouldn't make unfounded accusations."

I knew she wouldn't like the question, but I had to

ask, "Was there any problems between Lyon and your husband? Or your husband and Hoffman?"

She glared at me. "None whatsoever. Lyon and Fred were the best of friends. They stood up for each other. They never would fight over a competition let alone anything else."

Bitsy licked Dorothy's chin.

"And Hoffman?"

"My husband and I didn't approve of his tactics. My husband was quick to let him know how egregious his actions were, but we never had any problems with him. Now I have to get Bitsy ready for Best in Show." She turned her back to me, set Bitsy on the table, and went to brushing her.

I had offended her but decided to leave quietly and let her calm down.

CHAPTER 12

*J*udging for the Working Group was starting in five minutes. I decided to go and watch the competition. Ina's mastiff would be competing along with the Saint Bernard who beat out Paw. The spectator benches had begun to fill, but I found a seat three rows up. Ina's friend and fellow mastiff owner, Alex, sat down next to me. We smiled at each other, then watched as the dogs lined up.

Ina looked fabulous in a deep-plum outfit, and her mastiff's fur was groomed to perfection. They moved together as one to their place in line.

The judge was the same one who had judged Paw yesterday. She nodded to an assistant who stood back as the judge took a walk down the line of competitors. Besides the mastiff and Saint Bernard, there was a Newfoundland, a Great Dane, a Rottweiler, and several other breeds. Once the judge walked past everyone, she returned to stand beside her judging platform. She signaled for the first dog to step forward.

The judge followed the same routine that she used when judging Paw. She examined the dog then observed the gait and movement of the animal as the dog and owner ran back and forth in the ring. One more quick examination and the competitors went back to the line-up.

Ina was the second to be judged. Once again, she did beautifully. Two others competed before the Saint Bernard, who did splendidly.

I sighed, wishing Paw would do so well. I admonished myself in the next breath, though. It would be fantastic to win a dog show, but I wouldn't change Paw for the world. I was happy with him as the lovable mutt he was.

The final competitors finished, and the judge asked the entire line-up to walk around the ring. She observed intently then signaled everyone to stop and wait. Her assistant brought a record book to her, and they consulted for a few minutes. Then she began pulling dogs out of the line-up and arranging them in a new order. She went down the line pointing out first place, second place, and so on.

Alex and I clapped loudly, and Alex whistled enthusiastically as Ina and her mastiff won. The Saint Bernard had taken second place, and her owner shook hands with Ina, happily congratulating her. If he had hard feelings about losing, he didn't show it. The other competitors surrounded Ina, congratulating her. Everyone respectfully thanked the judge as well and let her speak with Ina.

I waited on the sidelines to congratulate Ina. Across the ring, I saw Jed Gray. He was frowning in my direction. I looked behind me to see if it was me or someone else. Various people milled behind me, including Dorothy talking with the bloodhound owner. She must have come to see the judging. A little to her left I saw Matt chatting with the Newfoundland owner.

Alex spoke to me, and I forgot about Jed. "I hear you found Hoffman last night."

"Yes. I did."

"It's terrible what happened to him. I never liked the guy, especially after he belittled Ina, but murder is just wrong."

"Any idea who would want to kill him?"

"Just about everyone." He sighed. "Ina would say that I shouldn't say that. She tries to find the good in everyone, but no one liked the guy. He was brash and unethical. I wouldn't be surprised that someone caught him tampering with their dog or equipment and killed him for that."

I saw Ina beginning to walk toward us. I hurried to ask Alex two more questions before Ina got there, for she would admonish him not to speak ill of the dead.

"Alex, what about the judge Hoffman accused of bias? Do you think he would kill Hoffman?"

"You mean Ken Topelo? I doubt it. He's level-headed and calm. It is not the first time competitors have complained and overreacted. I'm certain the committee will back up his judging decision. Of course, Lyon Connors complained about him a year ago, and too many complaints can go against a judge, but still it seems unlikely he would kill over it."

Ina was getting closer, so I quickly asked, "Connors complained about Topelo?"

"Yes. It was the same type of situation. Connors claimed Topelo favored one of the other entrants over him. Nothing came of it. Everyone else sided with Topelo."

"Who was the entrant who won?"

Alex shrugged. "I don't remember."

I had the feeling he just didn't want to say. I had time for one more question before Ina joined us. "I heard someone put in a complaint against Hoffman. Did you hear anything about it?"

"Really. Someone complained?" He laughed. "I'd love to know who did it. That would have served him right to face a complaint. I almost wish he was still alive to face it."

I looked at him sharply.

"Easy, amiga," he said. "I didn't like the guy, but I didn't kill him."

I wished I could believe that, but I wasn't ruling anyone out.

Ina had reached our side. Alex smiled at her. "Ina, my love. You did splendidly. Congratulations my friend." He kissed her cheek and hugged her then reached down to Max, her mastiff, and scratched his head. "You, too."

I congratulated Ina on her win. She smiled warmly. Then I patted Max's head, telling him he was handsome. He grinned with his tongue hanging out the side of his mouth.

Alex gestured to me. "We were just discussing Hoffman's murder. Clarissa found the body."

Ina gasped. "How horrible." She drew Max closer to her side.

I shuddered at the memory. "It was a shock. Fortunately, my friends were with me."

"I can't believe anything like this would happen at one of our shows."

"Alex and I were discussing who would want to kill Hoffman. Do you know if he had any enemies?"

Ina grimaced. "I would like to say no one, but Hoffman had an abrasive personality that angered a lot of people. But to kill him? I still find that hard to believe."

"Anyone, in particular, he angered or argued with? At this show or in the past?"

"I think he must have argued with everyone at the shows at least once. That includes me. Two years ago, he accused me of using a choke collar on Max here. I hadn't, of course. He saw me with one and assumed I used it. The fact was that I had taken it off a new competitor who was using it on his Rottweiler. I reported him to the show officials. They backed me up when Hoffman complained, but he never apologized for yelling at me and falsely accusing me. I decided to look at it as he at least cared enough about the dogs to treat them humanely."

My eyes widened. "Wait a minute. Hoffman didn't use a choke collar?"

"No. He never did or would. Why do you ask?"

"Because I saw..." I stopped myself before saying that I saw one in his hotel room. No way could I explain that without incriminating myself. "...him with one and he had a red choke collar around his neck when we found him." I thought a moment. "I think it must have been the same one. I just assumed it was his."

Alex put his arm around Ina's shoulders. "No. I agree with Ina. He abhorred them. He was always adamant that the best way to train a dog was by hand signals and voice commands."

I thought about that. "Do you know anyone who does use them?"

Ina shook her head. "No. They are banned from the shows, and no one I know would use them."

Alex nodded. "I agree." He scratched Max's ears. Max closed his eyes in bliss.

Behind me, I could hear Matt's voice as he spoke to two of the other competitors.

I needed to speak with him. I said to Ina, "I better go and let you prepare for Best in Show."

Alex smiled. "She's going to do brilliantly."

Ina blushed. "I don't know about that. We'll see you later, Clarissa."

They waved then walked away. I turned around and

approached Matt. I was in luck for the other two competitors were leaving as I came up to him. "How is Lila?"

"She's doing well."

"No ill effects from last night's excitement?"

He smiled. "No. She's in excellent health. How is your dog?"

"He's fine. It takes a lot to affect Paw."

Matt leaned forward. "Do you know what happened to the mastiff?"

"He's with Paw right now. Shelbee took charge of him, and he has settled down."

"That's good. I hear Shelbee has a natural way with dogs."

"She does."

Matt tilted his head to where Dorothy stood talking to several other competitors. "She looks well this morning."

"Yes, she is."

"Did she say what happened?"

"Apparently, she went to the closet for a broom, and someone shoved her into the closet from behind and locked the door." I observed Matt for his reaction. His face remained blank.

"Does she have any idea who did it?"

"Not really. She thought she smelled perfume, but I wonder if she imagined it under stress."

Matt massaged his neck with one hand. "Perfume? That would mean a woman pushed her?"

"Or a man wearing perfume. It could have been cologne, too, I suppose."

Matt's hand stilled on his neck. "And she had her dog with her? Odd."

"What do you mean?" I hadn't thought it unusual.

"I would have left Lila in her cage while I went for a broom. It wasn't that far from her stall, right?"

I glanced over at Dorothy. She was holding Bitsy in her arms. She was really attached to the little Pomeranian. I felt a twinge of guilt for leaving Paw alone.

Matt looked over too. "She is devoted to that dog. I admit that I'm not as close to Lila since she's my aunt's dog."

Colby joined us. I noticed she wore a light floral scent, but waited to mention it.

I asked them, "I was wondering when Hoffman was killed. I figure it was between five and eight p.m. I left the hall at five, and there were a lot of people still here. Do you guys know when the hall emptied?" I made a mental note to ask Dorothy what time it was when she went to the closet.

Matt and Colby exchanged glances. Colby didn't seem surprised by my question, so I figured Matt had told her everything that had happened last night. I know Bruce would have told me.

Colby shrugged. "Matt went up to our room shortly after five. I know because I checked my watch. I was waiting for one of the spectators to come look at one of the puppies. Matt took Lila up since she's not always happy to see others handling her pups. The guy was to arrive at five fifteen, but he never showed. I waited until five thirty and then took the pups and went up to the room."

"Was the hall full of people at five thirty?"

"Not really. There were still many of the show participants wandering around, but the public had all cleared out. I did see a few people I knew. Jed Gray wandered by, and I saw Ina Holmes and Alex Cortez walk past the stall. Of course, the hall is huge; you can't see everything. I have no idea how many people were over by the vending stands."

Her comments reminded me of two things: I realized I needed to talk with Ina and Alex again, and I should question the vendors whose stalls were near the crime scene.

I was considering my next question when I felt a presence behind me. I turned to see Detective Gibbons standing there staring at me. She shifted her focus to Matt and Colby.

"Ms. Gerard?"

"Yes."

"Can you identify this object for me?" The detective held up a plastic bag containing a chain necklace with a pendant attached. The pendant was approximately a half-inch long, silver-colored dog.

"Oh, my goodness, that's my necklace. Where did you find it?"

"Ms. Gerard, I'm going to need you to come with me for questioning."

A uniformed officer that I hadn't noticed stepped behind Colby.

Colby glanced at her. "Why?"

Gibbons had a hint of steel in her voice. "I need you to answer questions in regards to this necklace."

Colby protested, "But I already told you it was mine."

The conversations from those around us had stopped, and everyone was listening intently to the conversation between Colby and Detective Gibbons.

Detective Gibbons started to turn away. "I have more questions to ask you. Now please come with us."

Matt stepped in front of the detective. "You still haven't told us why you need to ask Colby questions or where you found her necklace."

Detective Gibbons huffed. "It is a police matter and confidential."

"If you won't tell us, then I'm coming with you."

Detective Gibbons grimaced. "Suit yourself, but you will stay outside while I speak with her."

This time Gibbons stepped around Matt and strode away with Colby and the officer following her.

Matt hurried on behind.

Once they were out of hearing range, everyone around me began murmuring and talking excitedly.

I noticed Dorothy walking off with Jed Gray. I thought about catching up with them but decided to follow Detective Gibbons. Maybe I could learn some-thing more.

The detective was a fast walker, forcing me to run to catch up. The detective led Colby into the same stall she used last night to interview me. The uniformed officer blocked the entrance forcing Matt to stay outside.

I tried to listen to any words as I casually walked past, but the noise from all the people in the hall prevented me from hearing anything Colby or Gibbons said.

Matt paced back and forth outside the stall.

Since I wasn't having any success here, I decided to find Bruce. Perhaps he could find out more from his acquaintance, Sergeant Bull. I had yet to see or meet the Sergeant. I was heading to the front desk to page Bruce when a hotel clerk stepped in my path.

CHAPTER 13

*H*e was in his early twenties with short black hair and a thin build. Dressed in the hotel's standard uniform, he had a mischievous grin on his face. "Mrs. Brantford?"

"Yes."

"Your dogs are barking loudly again in your room. Could you please quiet them?" He continued to grin. Apparently, some of the staff were quite amused by Paw's antics.

I sighed. "Of course, I'll go right up."

Behind me, I heard Detective Gibbons instruct Matt to go somewhere else and stop pacing. Turning, I saw that she had stepped out of the stall.

Behind her, Colby nodded to Matt to go. I heard her say, "It's okay. You better check on Lila."

I saw Matt nod reluctantly and wander my way.

Detective Gibbons stared hard at me then returned to

the stall. I had the impression she didn't like me too much.

I wasn't sure I liked her either.

"Please, ma'am." The hotel clerk indicated I should get moving. I nodded to him and walked out of the hall.

A queue of people was waiting for the elevators, so I took the stairs. Once again, I vowed to start an exercise routine. Several flights of stairs were tiring me out. I knew Shelbee would be happy to see me exercise more.

I exited through the stairwell door to a quiet hall. I heard a room door close further down the hall as I came through the stairwell door. I guess not everyone was at the show. Paw and Samuel were barking loudly.

I hurried down the hall and opened our hotel door. Both dogs eagerly greeted me with wagging tails. It was good to see Samuel happy. I grabbed leashes, snapped them onto the dogs' collars, and checked the lock on the door as both dogs pulled me forward, ready for some action. I hesitated to walk both since they each would be a challenge to control, but if I left one alone, the barking would continue. Choosing to walk them both, I took the elevator down instead of the stairs. I could see myself falling head first down the stairs if they went that way. Paw would never intentionally hurt me, but I was no match for two excited dogs.

The elevator opened, and Matt stepped out. We nodded to each other as he walked past me, preoccupied with whatever thoughts were on his mind. Fortunately, no one else was in the elevator. The three of us stepped in, filling up most of the space. The elevator descended to the lobby. I exited the elevator, holding tight to each leash, planning to take the dogs out to the dog park the hotel had provided.

We were heading across the lobby to the side entrance when I spotted Jac coming through the front doors. She carried a tote bag over her shoulder. I waved to her, and she walked over to us, patting both dogs when she got to my side.

"Hey," I said. "That didn't take long. How's your dad?"

"He's fighting with the plumbing in the house again, cursing and loving the work at the same time." Jac laughed. "He loves our mysteries too, so he urged me to return and tell you to be careful. I grabbed a few things and hurried back. I don't want to miss out on this investigation, either. How's it going?"

I updated her on everything I had done and witnessed so far this morning.

She listened intently. "Have you told Bruce or Shelbee about Colby?"

"No. I was going to find them when the hotel clerk told me about the dogs barking. I had to hurry and quiet them. I plan to walk Paw and Samuel then go find Bruce and Shelbee."

Both Paw and the mastiff were straining at their leashes.

Jac grasped Samuel's leash. "I'll help you walk them."

Samuel accepted Jac's firm hold on the leash.

I was surprised at how quickly he had come to trust us.

We went out the side entrance and entered the dog park. The park was quiet with only a few other dogs and their owners in it. We walked the perimeter allowing the dogs to sniff and investigate at their own pace.

"I keep feeling like I am missing something obvious with this murder, but I can't think what it is."

"Don't be so hard on yourself. It has been a lot of upheaval in a short time. Yesterday you were learning how to handle Paw in the dog show ring and trying to find out who may have wanted Connors murdered. Now we've got a new murder and more suspects. It would confuse anyone."

I sighed, realizing she was correct. It had only been two days, even though it felt like two years.

"I wonder what triggered Hoffman's murder. I mean he was antagonistic to these people for years. Why kill him now?"

Jac adjusted her tote bag strap on her shoulder. "Maybe someone just got fed up with his bullying ways."

"Could be, but I get the feeling that it was more than that."

"You told me that Colby claims Matt went to their room at five and then she went up at five thirty. Maybe we should check with Ina and Alex to see if they saw her and find out if Matt really did go to his room."

"I agree plus I need to ask Dorothy if she remembers what time it was when she went to the closet. It would help narrow down the time frame for the murder. And how she got locked in the closet."

Jac snapped her fingers. Both dogs looked up at her. "That reminds me. Remember when the night manager unlocked the closet door. He mumbled something about where the block was. I wonder what he meant. And why have a closet that locks on both sides? Don't most closets only lock from the outside, if at all?"

My eyes widened. "Good point. I was so absorbed with calming Dorothy that I didn't give it a thought. We need to find that out."

Jac nodded. "Do you suspect anyone besides Matt and Colby?"

"I am suspicious of Jed Gray. I didn't see him at all yesterday until after the murder. I feel we need to know where he was and what he was doing. Why did he show up right after the murder?"

"Was he scheduled to be in the show?" Jac pulled on Samuel's leash to keep him close.

He whined softly, eager to chase a squirrel sitting by one of the shrubs.

Paw sniffed at the grass by my feet, ignoring the squirrel.

"I thought so. He claimed to have shown his dog, Tuck, early in the day but failed to win his breed competition. I better ask around and see if he did show his dog. That might answer where he was, at least for part of the day."

"Let me check on that. I will question the dog owners surrounding his stall to see if he was there yesterday."

"Good idea." The dogs had sat down at our feet, having finished inspecting the area. "Let's get these two back inside and find Shelbee and Bruce."

As we walked back to the lobby, Jac asked me, "Do you suspect Ina or Alex?"

I was startled by the question. "I hadn't thought of them as suspects," I admitted. "I've been concentrating on the others, but that may be naive. I'll check on their whereabouts. Anyone else you think we should check on?"

"I think one of us should check on the show judge Hoffman accused."

"Yes. I agree. That reminds me, I'd like to know who lodged the complaint against Hoffman and what it was about."

"Shelbee knows a lot of the judges. I bet she could find out."

I nodded in agreement as the four of us entered the lobby.

Samuel woofed excitedly and lunged forward, ripping the leash from Jac's hand.

Paw thought this was a good idea and pulled the leash from my hand. Both dogs ran toward the elevators to our right, hidden by a corner.

Jac and I ran after them. Before either Jac or I could turn the corner, we could hear Shelbee laughing and talking to the dogs.

I skidded around the corner to see the mastiff presenting his belly for a rub while Paw swapped Shelbee's legs with his energetic tail.

I grabbed Paw's collar while Shelbee finished Samuel's belly rub and picked up his leash.

Jac smiled at Shelbee. "He trusts you."

I stared down at Samuel. "It's good to see him happy."

Shelbee cooed, "He's a good boy."

Paw barked for attention.

Shelbee and Jac laughed.

I affectionately rubbed Paw's ears. "Come on, you big ham."

Both dogs' ears perked up as their heads turned in unison toward the sound of the descending elevator. Paw and Samuel began barking at the elevator doors.

I sighed. "Now what?"

Behind me, I heard hurried footsteps. "Keep those dogs quiet!"

A man dressed in a suit rushed up to us.

I had expected the night manager. "Who are you?"

Both dogs continued barking.

The man's mouth dropped open for an instant. He recovered, saying, "I'm the hotel manager, Mr. Jackson."

I frowned. "You're not the manager from last night."

He nodded. "No, ma'am. I'm the day manager. Now please control your dogs' barking."

Shelbee was trying to calm the dogs but with little success. Something about the elevator had them agitated. Both had ridden in it several times with no problem. I noticed Jac had her head tilted, listening as the elevator reached the hotel lobby. She, too, seemed to hear something disturbing.

The elevator doors opened to reveal Lila, the Chihuahua, yipping, barking, and dancing in circles. She looked at us and launched into a loud vocal lament. Paw and Samuel understood for they increased their volume and tugged at their leashes to get onto the elevator.

"Now see here ..." the manager began but was cut off by a new voice.

"Lila!" Colby cried. She hurried to us, trying to catch Lila, who had been weaving around our feet.

I got the impression that Lila was trying to herd us into the elevator. The doors began to close with Paw and Samuel inside.

Jac reached out and stopped the doors from closing.

Behind Colby, Detective Gibbons and another officer approached. The detective assured the manager that she would handle the situation.

By now, Lila was in the elevator with Paw and Samuel. They were barking incessantly.

Detective Gibbons yelled over the noise, "Can't you get them to shut up?"

I raised my voice. "I think they want us to follow them."

The detective blinked in confusion. "Follow them? Where?"

Jac stepped on the elevator, saying, "Why don't we find out?"

Shelbee and I followed with Colby squeezing in too. There was no room left for the detective or her companion.

I yelled to them as the doors closed, "Third floor." The last I saw, the detective was scowling at me.

The elevator ascended slowly. Lila jumped up and down eager to lead us. As soon as the doors opened on the third floor, Lila rushed out, running down the hall.

The door to the stairwell banged open as Gibbons and her companion ran through it. The detective wasn't even breathing hard, but her companion was.

I sighed to myself. At least I wasn't the only one who needed to get in shape.

Lila stood a third of the way down the hall, barking at us.

Paw and Samuel ran to her.

She stood in front of a hotel room that's door stood open. She ran into the room with both dogs following her.

Colby ran after them, crying, "That's our room!"

We were right behind her. We reached the room in time to see Colby kneel next to a man lying unconscious on the floor. Lila was licking his face. Paw sniffed around the man while Samuel moaned in agitation.

It was Matt lying on the floor. Was he dead?

Shelbee must have had the same concern for she knelt and felt for a pulse. "He's alive."

Everyone in the room released a collective sigh of relief.

Matt groaned and began to stir.

Shelbee stepped back and hugged Samuel to calm him.

Paw continued to sniff around the room.

Matt half sat up, gingerly touching the back of his head. "What happened?" he asked in confusion.

Gibbons placed a hand on his back. "We were hoping you could answer that."

Matt tried to shake his head as if to clear his confused thoughts, but he winced at the movement.

I crouched in front of Matt. "It would be a good idea to have a doctor check you over."

A voice from the door said, "The doctor is assisting with a birth."

I turned to see who was speaking. The manager stood in the doorway.

Shelbee nodded to the detective. "I could get Sal to look at him. He's a vet, but he will know if Matt needs medical attention."

The detective stood up. "Where is he?"

"I just saw him in the hall. He has a vendor stand there."

Colby pleaded, "Please get him."

The detective nodded for Shelbee to go.

Jac took over comforting Samuel as Shelbee rushed out of the room.

The detective stood looking down at Matt. "What do you remember?"

Her companion had stationed himself by the door after allowing the manager into the room.

"I heard Lila yipping and barking as I neared the room, and I rushed in to open the door to get to her. Lila was scratching to get out of her cage. I've never seen her so frantic to get out of her cage. The next thing I know, I am surrounded by all of you."

"You didn't see anyone or sense anyone else in the room?"

"No."

"Your door was locked, correct?"

Matt began to nod but winced. "Yes."

Colby gasped. "Then how did anyone get in our room?"

Paw, nose to the floor, walked to Matt's side and sniffed the broken lamp on the floor. It was like the lamps in my room and the one I had seen in Hoffman's room. A standard issue hotel lamp with a heavy ceramic base.

The sergeant ordered, "Get that dog away from there! He's compromising a crime scene."

The detective added, "Take all three of the dogs out of here."

I thought of protesting that Paw was looking for clues but decided to let it go.

Colby was less inclined to listen. "Lila isn't hurting anyone," she said. "She's been upset and needs us with her."

"Nevertheless, they are in the way."

Colby looked like she was going to continue arguing, but Matt reached out and grasped her arm. "She'll be fine with the other dogs." He looked at me. "Can you take them to your room?"

"Of course." I called the dogs.

Paw reluctantly left the lamp as I pull on his collar. "You and the others have to go to our room for a while."

The other two willingly followed me after Paw woofed to them.

I could tell by the look on the detective's face that she thought I was crazy talking to Paw like he was human.

The sergeant just smiled in bemusement.

We walked across the hall where I opened the door and led the dogs inside. They wanted to follow me back out as I went to leave, but I told Paw they needed to stay for a while. He hung his tail dejectedly but lay down on the carpet.

I locked the door and turned around, nearly running into Dorothy.

She was peeking into Matt's room. In her hands, she held a basket of pet supplies. She jumped when I gasped.

CHAPTER 14

"*J*'m sorry, Dorothy. I didn't see you there."

"It's all right, dear. I admit I was distracted. What's going on?" She indicated the activity in Matt's room.

I could hear the detective continuing to question Matt. "You have no idea why someone would want to harm you?"

Matt answered, "No."

Dorothy's eyes widened. "He was attacked?"

"Apparently. He came into the room to check on Lila, and someone attacked him from behind."

"Just like me!" She shivered. Then she went into the room. Gibbons would not be happy about more people showing up in the room.

I started to follow her when I noticed Shelbee coming down the hall with a man in a Hawaiian print shirt and khaki pants. He carried a backpack.

Behind me, a voice said, "Looks like more excitement."

I turned to find Jed Gray standing right behind me. Where were all these people when Matt was attacked? I knew I needed to question Jed further, but it would have to wait.

Shelbee and the man, who I assumed was Sal, squeezed past us into the room.

I followed with Jed on my heels.

Colby was yelling at Dorothy. "Are you crazy? Why would I push you into a closet?"

"I have no idea. But you are wearing the same perfume as the woman who attacked me."

Colby had her clenched fists propped on her hips. "How on earth could you even know if it was the same perfume?"

"I worked on a perfume counter for years. I never forget a scent."

"I didn't push you, and I'm sure lots of other women at the show are wearing the same perfume."

Dorothy smirked. "I think not. That scent was discontinued some time ago. In fact, I'm surprised you are wearing it."

Colby nearly exploded. Matt was valiantly holding her arm as Sal was trying to examine Matt's head. "This perfume was my grandmother's favorite scent. I wear it in her honor. And I repeat, I didn't push you. Someone else must have been wearing the same scent."

So far, Detective Gibbons had watched this little

scene play out without interrupting. "Ladies, I would be interested to hear each of your observations." She stressed the word ladies. "Mrs. Hawkins, would you please go down to the hall to the police stand and wait for me. I will be down shortly to interview you."

Dorothy protested. "I have to get back to Bitsy. I left her alone, and she hates that."

The detective asked in confusion, "Bitsy?"

I smiled. "Her dog."

Dorothy sniffed. "She isn't just a dog. She's a champion with a sensitive nature."

Colby snorted.

Before Dorothy could argue her point, the detective said, "Go back to Bitsy. I assume she is at your stand in the hall?"

Dorothy nodded.

"Then wait there, and I will come and speak with you."

Dorothy nodded and left the room.

"Ms. Gerard, please accompany Sergeant Bull downstairs and give him your statement concerning Mrs. Hawkins's accusations." The detective motioned for the sergeant to escort Colby.

Colby opened her mouth, no doubt to protest, but Matt grasped her hand and said, "Go on. I'll be fine."

Silently, she followed the sergeant from the room.

The detective stepped to the door and examined its lock.

From where I stood, I saw no visible signs of tampering.

The detective turned to the hotel manager. "Mr. Jackson, have any hotel keys been reported missing?"

The manager blanched. "Er...ah... not that I know of."

"Then perhaps you should check."

"Yes. Right away." He turned to leave.

The detective stopped him. "I am sure I can count on your discretion in these police matters."

The manager straightened to his full height and puffed out his chest. "Of course." He stood for a moment then scurried out of the room.

Gibbons asked Sal, "How is Mr. Monroe's injury?"

"I want the hotel doctor to examine him as soon as possible, but I don't think he suffered any permanent damage. He'll have a wicked headache for a day or two, though." He looked at Matt. "I want you to get a scan to rule out a concussion. I don't think you have one, but it pays to be cautious. Have someone with you for the next two days. Pain medicine is fine. If you start to feel worse or have vision problems, find me, or the doctor, right away."

Matt tried to nod again and winced. "Thank you, Sal."

Gibbons nodded. "Yes. Thank you," (she hesitated) "Doctor."

"No problem." He smiled and stood up.

Matt still sat on the floor and he, too, tried to rise.

Sal steadied him and helped him to sit in a chair.

Jed stepped forward and offered to accompany Sal

downstairs. I hadn't noticed Jed's dog, Tuck, by his side until he jumped up on Sal's leg. "There's a good boy," Sal said as he petted Tuck.

Shelbee inserted herself between the two men. "I'll walk with you if you don't mind. Provided that is all right with the detective." She glanced over to Gibbons who nodded her consent.

Sal smiled at Shelbee, but Jed wore a frown.

Gibbons returned to questioning Matt. "Mr. Monroe. You said your dog was trying to get out of his cage? Did you unlatch it?"

Matt corrected the detective. "Her."

"Excuse me?"

"Lila is a she. She was trying to get out of her cage. I didn't let her out, though."

"Then how did she get out?"

"I don't know."

I cleared my throat. "Could whoever hit you have let her out?"

The detective looked at me in warning.

I was intruding, but I didn't care.

Matt shrugged. "Yeah, I guess. But why? Do you think they were trying to steal her?" He looked at me.

"I don't know."

The detective frowned. "Why would anyone want to steal your dog?"

I answered. "She is a show dog, and she has won championships. Correct?" I looked at Matt.

"Yes. Several."

"That makes her valuable. Could be someone wanted to steal her for the money. Or to hurt Matt."

Matt held up a hand. "Before you ask detective, I can't think of anyone who would want to hurt my aunt or me. Dog showing is her hobby, not mine. The only reason I am here being that my aunt broke her hip and couldn't show her dog herself. My aunt is well-respected, and I can't think anyone would want to hurt her."

I said, "There is another possibility. Someone could be trying to keep you from competing in Best in Show later today."

Gibbons shook her head. "Is this Best in Show that important?"

Matt and I spoke in unison. "Yes."

A young police officer stepped into the room. "Sergeant Bull sent me to secure the scene." In his hands was a roll of crime scene tape.

Gibbons motioned for him into the room. "Good." She addressed Matt. "Mr. Monroe. Please take a few minutes to check if anything is missing. Don't touch the lamp or dog cage. Once you do that, you'll need to leave your room until we are done collecting evidence."

Matt stood a little unsteadily and checked through his luggage and possessions.

Jac had been quietly observing the room. Now she said, "You can come across the hall and rest in Clarissa's room."

Matt sighed in relief. "Thank you." He finished his search. "I can't find anything missing."

Gibbons ushered us out of the room and gestured for the officer to cordon off the scene.

Jac took Matt over to our room where the dogs greeted him.

Gibbons motioned to me. "Mrs. Brantford, or should I say Ms. Hayes? I would like to speak with you a moment." The detective's tone indicated she would not accept a refusal.

We walked down the hall and stepped into the stairwell.

I frowned. "I suppose you spoke with Bruce."

"I have, and while I respect his position, I will not tolerate any interference in this investigation. I expect you to comply as well. The police will handle this matter."

I gritted my teeth. I had been around cops most of my life as my uncle was chief of police in our town. I knew they took their job seriously, and I admired that, but I was accustomed to attention and respect when I shared my observations.

"What if one of us comes across important information?"

"I would consider it, but let me stress that your information better not come from snooping. There is a killer on the loose, and I don't need civilians putting themselves in danger."

"Fair enough," I said, grinding my teeth. That said, she turned and walked down the stairs.

I fumed for several minutes but realized that it was counterproductive. Standing here wasn't the way to solve a murder. I wasn't about to give up on solving this case. I'd just have to avoid the police as much as possible.

Opening the stairwell door, I stepped back into the hall. Bruce was stepping off the elevator to my right.

We spoke in unison. "Where have you been?"

I growled. "I was being warned off the case by Gibbons. What about you?"

"Following a lead. Let's go to our room and catch up."

I reached out and grabbed his arm as he started to walk away. "Not a good idea. Matt is in our room with Jac and the dogs."

Bruce raised an eyebrow.

"I'll explain, but I don't imagine you want to discuss the case in front of him."

"No. I don't. Let's go down to the cafe."

"Okay."

We waited for the elevator in silence. I organized my thoughts. We had a lot to discuss. The elevator dinged, the doors opened, and we stepped on to descend to the hotel hobby. Once there, we exited and turned toward the cafe. It wasn't time for lunch yet, so the cafe was fairly empty. We chose a table away from the few other customers so we could talk in private.

The waitress arrived quickly. Bruce ordered coffee while I chose tea.

Bruce asked once the waitress had left, "So what has been happening?"

"I could ask you the same thing."

"You go first."

I proceeded to tell him of the attack on Matt and the confrontation between Colby and Dorothy. He listened without interruption. I stopped my recitation when the waitress returned with our coffee and tea. I finished by recounting my earlier conversation with Dorothy once the waitress had left.

Bruce mused out loud. "Why would anyone want to attack Matt?"

I stirred my tea to cool it. "I don't know. It appeared as if someone was after Lila unless that was a ploy to throw off suspicion for the real reason for the attack. If they were after Lila, it could be that it has no connection to the murder. Matt could have surprised the thief or saboteur in the act."

"We have to remember that Hoffman was accused of using similar tactics to win shows. Could he have had an accomplice who is still working to sabotage competitors?"

"To what end? Hoffman's mastiff is no longer in the show. Samuel didn't make it out of group, and unless the judge's ruling gets overturned, Ina is the winner of the Working Group competition."

Bruce gulped some coffee. "The ruling will stand. That's one of the things I learned this morning. I went to check into the judge Hoffman complained about. The officials have sided with the judge. Ina is the official winner of the mastiff competition. But if there was an accomplice, he or she could be seeking revenge for the competition loss."

"I still don't agree. If they wanted revenge, wouldn't they go after the judge or Ina, instead of Matt?"

"Could be they blame Matt for confronting Hoffman about the judge's ruling?"

I took a cautious sip of tea, careful not to burn my mouth. "Either way, we need to find out if Hoffman had an accomplice."

"We'll need to question everyone to find out if they knew of anyone Hoffman associated with," Bruce thought out loud.

"That's the problem. Everyone I have spoken to referred to Hoffman as someone who didn't get along well with others. No one mentioned a friend or acquaintance. Based on his personality, I can't see him working with another person."

Bruce drained his mug. "We will have to ask anyway."

"Do you think this is all connected to Connors's death?"

"My gut says yes."

"Then we need to find out what connects Connors, Hoffman, and Matt's attack." I continued to stir my tea. I couldn't understand how Bruce could drink such hot coffee.

"Plus, the attack on Dorothy and maybe her husband's death."

"I can see Hoffman killing Connors or even Dorothy's husband if he was killed, but why push Dorothy into a closet?"

Bruce shrugged. "It could have been to keep her out of the way for a meeting in the hall."

I sipped my tea. "A meeting that resulted in Hoffman's death. Why not kill Dorothy and leave her in the closet? The killer hasn't hesitated to kill when you consider Connors's and Hoffman's deaths."

"It may have been Hoffman who pushed her into the closet." Bruce put up his hand as I started to protest. "Or his accomplice, if Dorothy is correct about the perfume."

"Then Hoffman could have a female accomplice. But where was she when Hoffman was murdered? Or was she the killer?"

"We need to find out why Hoffman was in the hall. Was he meeting someone or was he lured there?"

Finally, I was able to take a full drink of my tea. "That's going to be hard to find out unless we can find a witness. Which reminds me, did you talk to Sergeant Bull and find out what the police have discovered?"

"No. He wasn't here this morning, but I checked out the mastiff judge's alibi. He was playing poker with two other judges during the time of the murder. I'll try to talk to Bull later this morning or early this afternoon."

I swallowed some tea. "I wonder who lodged the complaint against Hoffman. That could have triggered a confrontation that resulted in his death."

"I'll ask one of the show officials. If he refuses to tell me, I'm sure he'll tell Sergeant Bull."

I finished my tea. "The detective asked the hotel manager about missing keys. I wonder if keys are missing, and if so, do they have a connection to the closet keys?"

Bruce gazed into his empty cup. "Could be there is a master key. I'll ask some of the hotel staff."

"Do you think they'll tell you?"

"It's worth a try."

I shook my head. "Jac brought up a good point. She wondered about the closet's lock. Why couldn't Dorothy open it? Most closets only lock on the outside. Plus, Jac remembered the night manager mentioning a wooden block."

Bruce scratched his jaw. "Hmm. Now that you mention it, I remember him saying the same thing. I'll ask the staff about that. If they don't tell me, I'll mention it to Sergeant Bull or ask the other dog fanciers."

"Looks like we have more questions than answers and the show will be over in a few hours. It's going to be incredibly hard to solve once everyone leaves."

"Then we best make the most use of our time while everyone is still here."

We both looked up as Shelbee approached our table.

I asked her, "Any luck questioning Sal about that pill?"

She shook her head. "It was a standard sleeping pill. It could knock a dog out and even be deadly if an animal ingested too much. Sal says it is nothing incriminating, though, since he knows many dog owners take the pills themselves for show nerves. We'd have to prove Hoffman actually used them on a dog."

Bruce set down his coffee mug. "Not easy to do."

I rotated my mug on the table. "Blood tests?"

He shrugged. "Yeah. Maybe. Of course, I haven't heard of any dog having problems at the show."

"No. I haven't either."

Shelbee nodded to me. "There's more. Judge Gray says he'll talk to you about his absence yesterday if you promise to keep what he tells you confidential. I'm to take you to him if you agree."

Bruce drummed his fingers on the table. "Can we trust him?"

"I believe so."

I stood up. "I'll talk to him and keep it confidential, provided it has nothing to do with the murder."

Bruce waved us to go, saying, "I'll pay for our drinks."

CHAPTER 15

I followed Shelbee from the cafe and through the hall to a side room.

Sal met us at the door and ushered me inside. "Please come in." He smiled at Shelbee. "Thank you."

Shelbee nodded in return. "You're welcome." To me, she said, "I'll see you later."

I nodded, and Shelbee left.

Sal closed the door. I gazed around the room. It reminded me of the room that had held the complimentary breakfast service yesterday morning. This one was the same size and design but held an assortment of supplies for medical emergencies.

As I studied the room, Sal said, "This space is for the on-site veterinarian provided by the show. The hotel insisted on a vet to cover them from any liability. Right now, he is in the hall checking on a litter of cocker spaniels. He graciously allowed us to 'borrow' the room."

Judge Gray sat at a small table in the corner. Tuck sat at the judge's feet. The judge nodded to the chair across from him.

The judge sighed, addressing Sal, "You sure about this?"

"I trust Shelbee's judgment. She says we can trust Clarissa."

I glanced back and forth at both men. "I'm confused. Do one of you want to explain?"

The judge nodded. "I'll explain, but I want your promise to keep what I tell you confidential. You can't tell that detective boyfriend of yours nor your other friends. That includes Shelbee."

"So you trust Shelbee's judgment but don't trust her to keep your secret?"

"Sal trusts Shelbee. I withhold judgment for now. Either way, the fewer people who know about this, the better. Your promise?"

"I promise to keep your secret provided that it has no connection to the crimes committed."

He gestured for me to sit at the table. "That'll do. What I have to tell you has nothing to do with Hoffman's murder or Matt's attack." He looked again to Sal and who shrugged.

The judge clasped his hands in his lap. "As you know I am a retired judge. For forty years, I did my best to serve justice. Never married. Judges are held to a high standard and scrutinized constantly. They are expected to behave in an upright, traditional manner. And for those forty years, I did that, but a man cannot deny his true nature nor should he." He paused in thought and reached down to pat Tuck.

Sal came over and placed his hand on the judge's shoulder. "Our society is not a tolerant one."

I was beginning to understand what they were talking about but left them to continue.

Sal smiled. "Jed and I have been seeing each other for years. We always had to arrange meetings under the guise of the care of his dogs. The shows and vet care were perfect for disguising our relationship. Even now, we feel we both must keep it a secret. Two men in love with each other turn a lot of people to hate."

They both gazed at me, studying my reaction. They were worried where I stood on the issue of gay relationships.

I shrugged. "Gentlemen, I can assure you that I have nothing against your relationship. I don't care if you are gay. It is none of my business."

They both visibly relaxed.

To Sal, I said, "I assume Rebecca isn't your girlfriend?"

"Rebecca is a kind soul. She has been agreeable to playing her role as a girlfriend."

"Why the ruse?"

Sal laughed bitterly. "If my true relationship were known, my vet practice would disappear. As for a girlfriend, well, I have the unfortunate problem of attracting women. Not to sound arrogant, but a single, attractive man attracts a lot of offers from women. It was easier to have a girlfriend to shield me from the attention."

I frowned. "I thought you weren't any longer a vet."

"I still have my license, and I consult, but my new business would suffer too. I left my practice to start the pet supply business hoping it would let Jed and I reveal our secret. After all, he has retired. But the same people I interacted with as a vet now purchase my supplies."

The judge accused me. "You think we are overly sensitive? I suggest you listen to what your fellow dog owners have to say. I think you'll find that the majority of them aren't so tolerant."

I nodded my head. I had to admit that I was thinking they were overstating the intolerance, but I had never faced being different. My relationship with Bruce was looked upon fondly by everyone I knew. "I accept that I don't know anything about the intolerance you have faced." A thought occurred to me. "Did anyone at the shows discover your relationship?"

Sal and Jed looked at each other. Jed grimaced. "Hoffman suspected I was gay. He didn't know about Sal, though. He insinuated that if I continued in the shows, he would expose me."

I shook my head. "Why?"

"Tuck may look like he is getting old, but he is still a champion. Hoffman always wanted to win Best in Show. He wasn't above using any means he could to disqualify or remove a fellow competitor." The judge patted Tuck on his back.

"So you let him bully you?"

The judge exploded, "I was protecting my loved ones."

"How do you know he wouldn't expose you, anyway? Seems to me this is a strong motive for his killing." Of course, as soon as I said that, I realized I was in a room alone with two men who could be killers. My stomach flipped.

The judge growled. "I was a judge. I upheld the law not broke it."

Sal put both hands on Jed's shoulders. Sal defended Jed. "Jed did show Tuck in the bulldog competition. He didn't let Hoffman bully him. I told Jed that we needed to stand up to Hoffman even if my practice suffered."

I shifted in my chair. "Tuck didn't win his breed, though."

Judge Gray sighed sadly. "No. He didn't."

"So where were you yesterday after the bulldog competition? And at the time of the murder? You both disappeared for most of the day and showed up only after Hoffman's body was discovered?"

Sal smirked. "We went to a friend's house near here. He's out of town for the month and let us use it. It offered us the chance to have personal time if you get my meaning."

I sighed. "Any witnesses who saw you there?"

"Would you want witnesses?"

The judge crossed his arms. "We were discreet. No witnesses and it's a quiet neighborhood."

"I don't suppose you will tell me where this house is located?"

"No. You'll just have to trust us. Besides, we were back in time to see you, and your friends, race to catch the dogs when they ran into the elevator."

I sighed. I wasn't sure that I could trust them. "You're on the same floor as us?"

The judge smiled. "Yes. I am."

I left Sal and Judge Gray and went in search of Ina and Alex. Colby had said that they had walked by her stall last night. Perhaps they could confirm seeing her and at what time. I should have asked Jed about it, but I forgot. I would ask him later.

The hall was packed today. The Best in Show competition would be in a few hours. The group competitions still had to finish. I dodged around people, heading for the mastiff section. Before I got there, I found Ina and Alex in the Weimaraner section admiring a litter of puppies.

I waved to them. "Hey, guys."

Alex smiled. "Hey."

Ina glanced at me sideways. "Hello." She was holding a wriggling grey puppy who was determined to lick her face.

I laughed at the adorable puppy's antics. "I thought you only bred mastiffs?"

Alex tickled the puppy under its chin. "She does."

Ina adjusted the puppy in her arms. "My niece is looking for a dog. She wants a Weimaraner, so I promised to check out any puppies at the show." Ina turned her attention to the puppies' owner and began asking questions.

Alex smiled, asking, "Why do I get the feeling you have further questions?"

I smiled back. "Am I that obvious?"

"Not really, but I know you have a curious mind. Besides your detective boyfriend has been asking questions."

I frowned. "What makes you think Bruce is a detective?"

Alex laughed. "You can't hide much at these shows. Everybody knows everyone else."

"Somebody is hiding a murderous streak."

Alex sobered. "True. I suppose there are secrets here. Your boyfriend isn't a secret, though. For instance, I know he's not your husband. The show judges know, and one of them is a friend. He told me that you are a detective."

"Yes."

"Do you think I'm the murderer or Ina?"

"You could be."

He frowned.

I hastened to add. "But I don't believe you are murderers. I do think you can help me out by answering a question."

Ina had concluded her interview with the Weimaraner owner. "We would be happy to answer any questions you have, Clarissa."

Alex frowned.

Ina squeezed his arm and nodded her head.

Alex sighed and nodded his head in agreement.

I smiled at them. "I want to know what time you left the hall last night and who you saw."

Alex scowled. "You do suspect us!"

"No, I don't. I'm trying to establish where everyone else was last night."

Ina narrowed her eyes. "Everyone or just certain people?"

"Colby Gerard and Matt Monroe. Colby claims that Matt went to their room earlier than her. She stayed later and said that both of you walked past her stall. Did you see her?"

Ina nodded. "We saw her. I didn't see Matt, but Colby was in their stall when we left."

Alex agreed. "We left together to have any early dinner. Colby was in her stall, but there was no sign of Matt."

"Early dinner? What time did you leave the hall and pass Colby?"

Ina looked at Alex. "It must have been a quarter to five. We wanted to go to the cafe in the lobby, and since the tables fill quickly, we decided to eat before it got too crowded."

"And that's when you saw Colby?"

"Yes."

"Was the hall still busy?"

Alex closed his eyes while he thought. "Most of the spectators were gone, but most owners were still in their stalls."

"And you went straight to the cafe? You didn't return afterward to the hall?"

Ina linked her arm through Alex's. "I went straight to the cafe to get a table. Alex took the dogs up to our rooms and joined me within a few minutes."

Alex explained. "We had the dogs with us when we passed Colby."

"Did you see Matt when you took the dogs up?"

"No."

"How about after you ate?"

"I walked Ina to her room, then went across the hall to mine. I stayed there for the rest of the night."

Ina shrugged. "Same with me."

"Two more questions?"

Alex rolled his eyes.

"Was anyone else with Colby when you saw her?"

They shook their heads in the negative.

"Okay. Last question. Did either of you see Jed Gray around that time or near Colby?"

Alex turned to Ina. "I didn't, did you?"

She thought a moment. "I don't recall seeing him all day."

Alex raised an eyebrow. "Will that do? Ina has to get ready for Best in Show."

"Yes. Thank you. Best of luck in the competition."

Ina smiled as Alex patted her arm and turned her back to the mastiff section.

Colby had told me that Matt had left at five and she had left at five thirty, but if Alex and Ina were correct, then Colby lied to me. She had claimed that they had walked past her as did Jed Gray. I was going to have to speak to Jed again and confront Colby.

CHAPTER 16

$\mathcal{I}$ wove through the crowds, headed back to the room where I had met Jed and Sal. Over the noise of the crowd, I heard the announcer broadcast the winner of the last group competition.

"The Best in Show will be delayed until 2 PM."

I wondered what had delayed it since it had been scheduled right after lunch. Time was running short, and I was glad for the delay in the show. Somehow, we had to solve this murder before all the owners went home.

Could Colby be the killer? Her necklace was found at the scene. Perhaps she and Hoffman had fought, and in the struggle, her necklace came off. Had she grabbed the shovel and hit Hoffman? Would he have had his back turned to her? I realized that the scene had confused me. Hoffman was hit from behind, and yet boxes across from the dog food display were all over the floor. Would someone turn their back to a person with whom they had just fought? Or were the boxes pushed over in a fit of anger? Hoffman was a tall, fit man. Both Jed and Sal were too. Jed was older than the other men, but he still seemed fit. Matt wasn't as tall as Hoffman, but he was strong.

Distracted by my thoughts, I rushed through the door where I had met Jed and Sal. I startled the only occupant of the room. He was of medium height with light brown hair.

It took him a moment to react. "Can I help you?"

I hesitated. "I'm looking for Judge Gray and Sal. They were here a few minutes ago."

He smiled. "I don't know about the judge, but Sal just left. Do you need medical help?"

I stared at him blankly. *Medical help? Do I look like I need medical help?*

He extended his hand. "Hal Stevens. I'm the on-site vet. Does your dog need help?"

I shook his hand. "How do you know I have a dog?"

"I just assumed since you rushed in here that you needed vet help. You do have dog hair on your clothes."

I laughed. "I do, and I do have a dog, but he is fine. I needed to talk to the judge and Sal on a different matter. You don't happen to know where they went, do you?"

"Sorry. No idea."

"I better go find them. It was nice meeting you."

"A pleasure."

~

I searched the hall as best I could. No sign of Jed or Sal. I passed the stall the police had commandeered. No one was in it. I decided to return to our rooms. Perhaps Matt was still there. I vowed to find out where he and Colby were last night. I wanted to catch him before he competed in the last competition.

Paw came to greet me as I walked in the door. He stood up, put his paws on my shoulders, and woofed in my face. I had been ignoring him, the woof said.

"I know big guy. Things have been kind of crazy. I promise you lots more attention soon."

He jumped down to the floor and rolled over on his back.

I spent several minutes rubbing his belly.

Jac sat cross-legged on the bed with Samuel beside her. He had his head on his paws looking wistfully at Paw and me. Poor guy. Only yesterday his owner was alive. Now he must feel like an orphan.

Matt wasn't there.

Jac read my mind. "He took Lila back to the hall."

I had observed the crime tape across his hotel door but had seen no activity around his room.

"The police done?" I nodded my head toward the door, indicating Matt's room.

"I guess. I think he was worried about Colby though. To be fair, the competition is just after lunch, so he needed to get ready."

I stood up. "Not anymore. The officials moved it to two o'clock."

"Why?"

"I don't know. I heard it announced in the hall a few moments ago."

The door knob rattled. Shelbee entered with Bruce right behind her.

She glanced at me. "There you are. We were looking for you."

Bruce closed the door. "How did it go with Judge Gray and Sal? Learn anything?"

"Yes and no. I agreed to keep confidential what they told me."

Bruce frowned, but I continued, "I can say that they both claim to have been away from the hotel all day."

Bruce began to open his mouth.

I put up my hand. "I promised confidentiality so I can't tell you where Jed and Sal went or why. For that matter, I don't know where they were. In my mind, they continue to be possible suspects."

"You said you did learn something, though."

"Yes. I spoke with Alex and Ina again. They left the hall last night around four forty-five, which is earlier than Matt said he left. They didn't see him, but they did see Colby. As I recall, Colby claimed to have seen them after Matt went up to his room. I came back here to talk to him, but Jac says he left to prepare for Best in Show."

Bruce asked Jac, "Did Matt say anything to you?"

Jac shrugged. "He is sure someone was trying to hurt Lila. I asked him why he thought that and he swears it is to remove her from the final competition. I asked him who he suspected. He wouldn't say, but if you ask me, it would have to be one of the others in the Best in Show."

Bruce began to pace. "We need to question the other group winners and find out where they were when Matt was attacked."

Shelbee sat on the couch. "But only half of the group competitions were complete at the time of the attack."

I sat cross-legged on the floor. "Could one of the other owners have acted to remove Lila because she tied with Dorothy's Pomeranian? I mean a tie is highly unusual. It adds one more dog to compete against in the final competition."

Paw joined me, curling up next to me.

Shelbee nodded. "It is highly unusual."

Jac stroked Samuel's ears. "Are you thinking Dorothy would do something like hurt Lila to win?"

I shook my head. "No. I can't see Dorothy hurting Lila. She dotes on Bitsy."

Shelbee observed, "All the dog owners dote on their dogs."

I caressed Paw's back. "True. I find it hard to believe any of them would harm another dog, but we know it has happened in the past."

Jac tilted her head in thought. "If we assume that someone was trying to harm Lila to disqualify her from the competition then what about the dog owners who hadn't finished competing in their groups? Do we consider them suspects? Even though they hadn't won yet?"

I sighed. "That's a lot of people to question in a short time."

Bruce stopped pacing. "We need to focus on the murder."

"You don't think the two are connected?"

"I do, but the murder comes first. I have no idea why the murderer would go after Lila, but we'll waste time pursuing that line of questioning. We need to concentrate on where our murder suspects were at the time of Hoffman's murder."

"Then we need to talk to Matt, and we need to remember that it's possible Lila wasn't the target. Matt could have been attacked because he knew something about the murder."

Bruce resumed pacing. "Or was involved in it."

Shelbee leaned forward. "Dorothy accused Colby of pushing her into the closet. What if Colby and Matt committed the murder together?"

Bruce paused in mid-step. "See, we need to find out where they were and why Colby lied about it."

My hand stilled on Paw's back. "Could the scene in Matt's room have been staged? Was Matt attacked?"

Shelbee said, "Sal swore Matt was injured."

I thought about that. "Then we need to find out if any hotel keys are missing. If the attack was real, then somehow someone got into Matt's room. Gibbons ordered the hotel manager to find out if keys were missing. I wonder what he discovered."

Bruce tapped his foot. "I'll look into it."

Jac asked, "What time is it?"

Shelbee looked at her watch. "Twelve o'clock. If you plan on questioning Matt and Colby, you'll have to wait until the Best in Show is over. They will be too busy getting ready for the competition in an hour."

I stood up, rousing Paw. "No, they won't. The competition has been pushed back to two o'clock."

"Why?"

"I don't know. I just heard it announced in the hall. Something to do with unforeseen circumstances."

Bruce cleared his throat, grinning. "I talked with Sergeant Bull. He arranged to have the competition delayed for an hour to give the police more time. Helps us too."

"Did you ever find out who complained about Hoffman to the judges?"

"No, but Sergeant Bull has agreed to ask the judging officials in his official capacity."

Jac moved to the edge of the bed. "Do you think that complaint was the reason for Hoffman's murder? I thought you believed it was connected to Connors's death. How could they be related?"

I shrugged. "I'm not sure if the complaints are related. I figure we need to find out who complained to determine if it is one of our current suspects, or if, we need to consider someone else."

Shelbee walked over to Samuel who had roused when Jac had moved. "You know, they could be connected."

"How so?"

"We suspect Hoffman of cheating in the show and lots of people have told us how Connors would do anything to win. Whoever complained could be getting back at Hoffman for causing them to lose a competition. That same person could have killed him and Connors in a grudge."

Jac stood up so Shelbee could sit by Samuel. "Would someone really go that far?"

I considered. "I would say yes from what I have heard from the other owners. Some competitors are deadly serious about winning."

Jac muttered, "Emphasis on deadly."

Paw woofed at her in agreement.

Samuel cocked his head to the side as if he were considering her words, then he sighed and laid his head down on his paws.

Jac said to him, "Shame you weren't there. You could lead us to the killer."

He looked up at her with sad eyes.

Bruce rubbed his neck. "Colby had a grudge against Connors. His accusations hurt her reputation and lost her dog sitting clients."

Jac said, "Matt probably held a grudge. Wouldn't you if your girlfriend was accused unfairly?"

Bruce gazed at me, his eyes softening. "Yes."

I smiled at Bruce.

Paw nudged my side seeking attention.

I scratched behind his ears.

Shelbee suggested, "We better hurry if we're going to

question Colby and Matt. The closer to the beginning of Best in Show the less likely we'll be able to talk to them."

Bruce nodded. "Agreed. Clarissa and I will talk with them."

Bruce and I moved to the door.

Samuel jumped off the bed. He and Paw hurried to the door, wagging their tails eagerly. We weren't getting out of the room without them.

Bruce and I agreed to take the dogs with us.

"We'll meet you at the café for lunch," Jac said.

I grasped Paw's leash and opened the hotel door as Bruce followed behind me with Samuel on his leash.

Shelbee and Jac followed us.

Both dogs had their heads down, sniffing along the hall corridor.

The elevator doors opened as we neared them and Detective Gibbons stepped out. She halted when she saw us. "I trust that you aren't planning to involve yourselves in my investigation."

I smiled innocently. "Of course not." I gestured to the dogs. "Just taking them for a walk."

"It needs all four of you to walk them?"

Paw quietly growled.

I patted his back in reassurance.

Samuel assumed a guard stance.

Bruce placed his hand lightly on the dog's back. "We're going to lunch, detective."

"Lunch?" Gibbons queried.

"Yes. You know that meal that most people partake of at noon."

Gibbons frowned at his sarcasm. "I know what lunch is, Mr. Sever. Where will you be partaking of this lunch?"

Shelbee said, "The cafe in the lobby. They allow dogs at their outside booths."

Gibbons's voice dripped with sarcasm. "How accommodating."

Bruce gestured to Matt's room. "Are your officers still searching for evidence?"

Gibbons hesitated to answer, weighing her words. "We're finished. If you see Mr. Monroe, please inform him that he can use his room." She waited a moment and then headed down the hall, stopping to pull off the crime scene tape on Matt's door. She proceeded down the hall and stopped at a door on the left. She glanced over her shoulder at us.

We entered the elevator, and as I turned, I saw her knock on the door. It opened revealing Jed Gray, but the elevator door closed before I could see anything else.

We parted in the lobby. Bruce and I took the dogs to the hall which wasn't as crowded as earlier in the day. I assumed many of the spectators had left to have lunch. We walked through the aisles heading for Matt's stall. Many owners were settled in their stalls either feeding their dogs or taking a quick nap. No one wanted to miss the Best in Show competition.

Neither did I. "I find it odd that the police finished with Matt's room so quickly."

Bruce agreed. "My guess is they are trying to hurry just like us. Everyone is going to scatter once the show ends unless the police have good cause to demand they stay."

I nodded as I guided Paw around a woman carrying a Pomeranian.

Paw growled low in his throat, and the Pomeranian yipped at him.

The Pom's owner glared at me and stalked past.

I needed to ask Shelbee how to correct Paw's hatred of the breed. Fortunately, the neighbor who had the Pomeranian Paw had tangled with had moved out. Odd to think, I mused, that such a little dog could irritate a Saint Bernard.

We found Colby with Matt in his stall. Lila was standing in a small tub filled with soapy water. She was shaking all over.

Matt looked up at us. Seeing me staring at Lila, he said, "She hates baths."

I smiled. "Paw loves them, especially when he can shake himself, sending water everywhere. How are you feeling?"

Matt shrugged. "Okay. Got a headache, but Sal doesn't think I have any permanent damage."

"Did the hotel doctor check you out?"

"Yeah, he did. He wanted me to go to the hospital for a scan, but I told him it would have to wait until after the show."

Colby shook her head. "I told him to go, but he wouldn't listen."

Lila yipped in agreement.

Paw and Samuel raised their heads, staring at her.

Paw shifted his weight, so I reached down and stroked his ears. To Matt, I asked, "Have you remembered anything else?"

"No."

"You're sure you locked your door."

Colby interjected, "Of course, he did." She was arranging brushes and a hair dryer on the stand beside the tub.

I saw a familiar design on the back of one of the brushes. It was blue and white with the VanCoy logo of a dove. I had received a complimentary one in our hotel room. VanCoy, the pet supplier to the show, was obviously using them as a marketing ploy. Next to this brush was a set of dark blue brushes.

I bent to examine the blue ones. "Those are pretty."

Bruce huffed, no doubt in exasperation.

Colby smiled. "I love those brushes. They are part of VanCoy's premier line and a lot better than this one." She held up the complementary blue and white one.

I visually compared the brushes. "Do you always use your own equipment?"

Matt nodded. "My aunt insists on using the best. Most

shows have a sponsor that gives out supplies, but she claims those aren't as good."

Colby nodded. "She's right. I would always use the better brushes. It brings a healthier shine to their coat and is easier on their skin. I don't know of any show owner who relies on the cheap stuff."

I silently gulped and looked down at Paw. He had been curiously studying Lila in the tub. Paw loved to get a bath, especially when he could escape and have me chase him around the yard. I'd always used brushes that I bought from local pet stores. They were affordable and on a writer's pay that was a prime consideration. Now I wondered if I had been harming his skin. One more thing I would have to ask Shelbee about.

"Do all the other owners use these dark blue brushes?"

Bruce shifted his weight from foot to foot. He was anxious to get to our important questions, but I wanted to know about these brushes. Paw's health was important to me.

"This brush is one of several in the premier line. Most people I know use this particular brush. Not everyone has dark blue. You can customize them to whatever color you want. Many owners have a color theme for their pets and choose to have their supplies in the same colors."

Matt said to Bruce, "That's not really why you are here, is it?"

Bruce stared at Matt. "No, it isn't. We have witnesses who claim you left before five o'clock last night."

Matt sighed.

Colby jumped into the conversation before Matt could answer. "They are lying."

"Why would they lie?"

"Maybe they have something to hide."

Matt lifted Lila out of the tub, wrapping a towel around her. He hugged her to his chest. "Colby." She looked at him. "It's time to tell them the truth."

Colby opened her mouth, no doubt to argue.

Matt shook his head and spoke to Bruce.

"It's true that I left earlier than I said. It was probably around four thirty. I went up to our rooms to call a friend of mine. A reporter. I know in my gut that Hoffman was wrong to accuse Ken Topelo, the mastiff judge, of cheating. I decided to see if my friend would come and cover the story. Maybe he could expose Hoffman as a cheater."

I asked, "Could you prove he cheated?"

"No, but you saw the mastiff competition. Someone let that dog run free and Hoffman never once complained. Do you think he would have stayed quiet if he thought someone was trying to mess with a competition he was in?"

"You make a good point."

"He only complained when he didn't win. My aunt has known Ina for years. They are good friends. Ina won that competition honestly."

Bruce didn't relent. "Did your reporter friend agree to come to the show?"

"No. I couldn't reach him, so I called a few of our

mutual friends. He's out of town covering a news story and isn't expected back until Tuesday."

Paw was trying to crawl under the table. I adjusted my grip on his leash. "Did you leave your room after you made those calls?"

"No. I stayed there and played with Lila. She truly hates to see buyers with her puppies."

I looked down in the cage by the tub. Lila's puppies were crawling around over each other and playing.

Bruce asked Colby. "Do you have anything to add to your alibi?"

She grimaced. "I did stay until five thirty, but Ina and Alex walked by before five. Jed Gray did too. And the buyer never did show up, so I collected the puppies and went up to our room. I didn't see anyone who could okay my alibi since almost everybody had cleared out. I didn't kill Hoffman. I don't care what Dorothy says about me. I didn't push her into any closet. I didn't even know what closet she means. And I can't see how she can claim it was my perfume."

Matt dismissed us. "We've told you the truth. Now we need to finish getting Lila ready for the show."

Colby raised her hand. "Wait a minute. I want to know why are *you* asking so many questions. Are you just nosey? And how come we've never seen you at any shows before?"

Bruce sighed. "You haven't seen us because we've never been to the shows. I'm a private investigator, and we're here on a case. We believe that Hoffman's murder is connected."

I added, "We're here undercover."

Colby motioned to Paw who leaned against me. "Is that Saint Bernard even your dog?"

Affronted, I said, "Yes. He is mine."

Matt cuddled Lila. "You've never shown him before, have you?"

"No. This is his first show."

Matt smiled. "He did well for his first show."

I smiled, proud of Paw's accomplishment.

Colby questioned Bruce. "What I want to know is what your case is?"

Bruce stiffened. "I won't tell you that."

"But it has something to do with the show or the owners, right? Otherwise, you wouldn't be here."

"Yes."

Matt asked, "Do you think the attack on Lila and me is related?"

I nodded. "We think so."

Colby and Matt looked at each other, then at us. Matt spoke, "I can't say that we are happy about this secrecy, but if you can solve the murder we would feel better. It is frightening to think someone is targeting the owners."

Bruce gently tugged on Samuel's leash. "We'll let you get back to preparing for the show."

I called, "Best of luck."

They nodded at us as we walked away.

CHAPTER 17

*P*aw and Samuel were happy to be moving again. We were headed to the hall entrance to meet Shelbee and Jac at the cafe.

Bruce suddenly stopped. "There's Sergeant Bull. I need to find out if he learned who complained about Hoffman. Can you take Samuel with you?"

"Yes."

He handed over the leash and walked off toward the sergeant.

"Well guys, it looks like it's just the three of us. Let's go find Shelbee and Jac."

The mastiff's ears perked up at Shelbee's name. He turned his head, searching for her, confirming my belief in Shelbee's rapport with animals.

We were weaving through a group of people when a shout went up to our right. "Help! Please help! They are loose."

The attention of everyone in the vicinity concentrated on the direction of the voice. A loose dog at a show could be a disaster. Show dogs were well-behaved, but in unfamiliar surroundings with lots of people, they could get hurt, or unintentionally, hurt others. Several dogs loose would be a real problem.

I turned toward the right to see the extent of the problem and promptly laughed. The loose dogs were playful Saint Bernard puppies. I could see three of them frisking their way amongst the people in the aisle I was standing in. I suddenly sobered, concerned that the bystanders would injure the puppies.

Paw must have had the same thought because he jerked on the leash, eager to help the puppies. We ran toward the scene, pushing through people in the aisle. They were not happy.

"Hey!"

"Watch out!"

"What do you think you're doing?"

Several other dog owners were rushing to help as well. I ran to keep up with Paw while Samuel kept by my side. Paw reached the puppies first and corralled two of them between his paws. They wiggled and squirmed trying to escape from him. The third puppy sniffed at Paw then fell on his side to bat at Paw's legs. Several people had stopped to watch Paw with the puppies. I heard several "awws" from the crowd.

The owner of the puppies hurried up to us. "Thank you! Thank you!" She looked down at Paw and her puppies and smiled then frantically looked around. "Where are the others?"

A deep voice to my left asked, "How many are there?"

I turned my head to see who had spoken. The voice sounded familiar. I looked up at Colin Sikes standing next to me. He was the British guy who had competed with me in the Saint Bernard competition.

The woman searched the crowded floor. "Five."

Everyone began to look for the two missing puppies. Several people bent down to see under tables and through people's feet. A few even got down on the floor and crawled around looking for the puppies.

A cry went up further down the aisle.

"Did someone lose a puppy?" a jovial voice called out. Down the aisle came a rotund little man in a brightly colored coat. He was holding a wriggling Saint Bernard puppy in his arms.

I smiled at the sight.

The owner rushed to take the fourth puppy in her arms. That left one more to find.

Beside me, Samuel woofed. He ducked his head and crawled under a nearby table with a long cover over it. More gentle woofs sounded from under the table.

Paw woofed his encouragement as well.

The mastiff emerged, herding a puppy from behind with a nudge of his nose.

Colin laughed.

The owner motioned to a young girl in her stall who bent to take the puppy from Samuel. Together she and the owner retrieved their puppies from Paw. The owner motioned for me to accompany them into their stall.

I followed with the dogs.

To my surprise, Colin followed as well.

The owner gushed. "I can't thank you enough. My name is Letitia Duvall, and this is my niece, Lettie."

Lettie smiled shyly.

I smiled. "Nice to meet you both."

Letitia reached down to both dogs. "And you both deserve a reward because you are my heroes." She pulled two dog treats out of her pocket. She looked up at me for approval.

I nodded my okay.

Both Paw and Samuel gratefully devoured their treat.

Letitia smiled down at them, then looked at me. "Are you in the competition?"

Colin answered. "She competed in the Saint Bernard competition, Letitia."

I was surprised she didn't know that fact.

Both must have sensed my curiosity because Letitia explained. "My sister, Amanda Barrett, is the dog competitor. I just come to help her out." She sighed. "I hope she doesn't find out the puppies got loose. I'll never hear the end of it. My sister is a real stickler about doing everything perfectly."

Colin hugged Letitia. "Don't worry, I won't tell, and I'm sure Lettie won't either." Colin directed his dazzling smile at Lettie who goggled at him and blushed.

I rolled my eyes at Colin's flirtatiousness. "I won't tell, either."

Paw woofed.

"He says he won't tell either," I quipped.

Everybody laughed.

I pulled on Paw's leash gently urging him to get up. He was lying beside the crate where the puppies were playing. "I had better go. It was nice meeting you, Letitia. You too, Lettie."

Samuel had settled next to my feet. He stood up.

Paw reluctantly got up as well.

Lettie wore a shy smile while Letitia said, "Nice to meet you."

Colin followed behind me. "I have to get back to Pettie. I'll stop back before the end of the show."

Letitia said to him, "You're going to watch Best in Show, aren't you?"

"Of course."

"Then we'll see you there."

Colin smiled. "I'll look for you lovely ladies."

Letitia laughed while Lettie blushed.

I rolled my eyes once again.

We walked away with the dogs.

"You love to pour on the charm, don't you?"

"Am I charming you, Luv?"

I smiled mischievously. "Not me just every other woman you meet."

He laughed loudly. "I can see I must work harder to charm you."

A stern voice said, "And why would you be charming her?"

I turned and found Bruce standing in front of me.

Colin grinned wickedly. "Why not?"

"Because she's my wife."

Colin's smile sobered. "Then you are a lucky man; however, I've heard that the two of you aren't married, detective."

My mouth fell open. "What?"

"You both have spent a lot of time asking questions. The police talk to you." He tipped his head toward Sergeant Bull who was walking away.

Bruce crossed his arms. "That has nothing to do with you trying to charm Clarissa."

Colin continued to provoke him. "Doesn't it?"

I huffed. "Men!"

They both looked at me.

I pointed to Colin. "You flirt with everyone so stop trying to provoke him. And you," I pointed to Bruce, "do not own me."

I turned around and stalked off. Let them settle it.

Paw and Samuel happily trotted at my side.

I had blindly walked away with no clear idea where I was going, so I just followed in the direction the crowd was going. We weaved through various aisles passing breeds of dogs both large and small. I found myself in the Pomeranian aisle. I passed Dorothy's stall but didn't stop. I was in no mood to be civil to anyone. Paw gave a low growl. Dorothy was busily grooming Bitsy. I reminded myself to ask Shelbee about correcting Paw's dislike of Pomeranians. We passed two more Poms in the aisle. Paw growled every time.

I weaved through more people and turned with the crowd toward the vendor booths.

I stopped.

Several people grumbled as they were forced to move around me.

The crowd was heading to the area where we had discovered Hoffman's body.

I turned around to avoid upsetting Samuel.

Paw pulled me slightly to the right and stopped at a door, open a crack.

We were standing in front of the closet in which Dorothy had been locked.

Paw looked up at me and lightly woofed.

He wanted me to open the door.

I, too, was curious to investigate.

I pulled the doorknob and took a step, hitting something with my shoe.

A wooden wedge-shaped block propped the door open, preventing it from closing. I stepped around it, leaving it in place.

The interior of the closet was dim. I transferred Paw's leash to the hand holding Samuel's leash and used my free hand to search the wall by the door. When I felt the light switch and flipped it on, an overhead light bulb brightened the room. I stepped inside with both dogs. Shelves containing various cleaning supplies and paper towels covered the walls from floor to ceiling, jutting out about a foot. A space in the middle of the room was just large enough for me to stand in with both dogs. The corner between the door hinges and the shelves contained a water bucket, mops, and brooms.

Slam!

CHAPTER 18

$\mathcal{I}$ jumped and turned. The closet door was closed. My heartbeat accelerated. I hated small enclosed areas. Taking deep breaths, I calmed myself. Perhaps the door was unlocked, and the prop was an extra security measure.

Both Paw and Samuel were at the door sniffing the crack under it.

I took two steps and grasped the knob, turning it. It didn't turn. I tried again twisting the knob as hard as I could. No luck. By now I was beginning to panic. I could feel the walls closing in around me. I started to breathe heavily.

Two noses push against my hands.

I looked down to see both dogs staring up at me in concern. I stared into their dark, soulful eyes and began to calm. We were fine. I told the dogs it was all right.

Caressing their heads, I took several deep breaths. I

wondered if this was how Dorothy had felt when she was locked in the closet. It must have been terrifying for her with no one around to hear her in the closet. Or was it? Had she been terrified for a different reason?

I knew that I was uncomfortable in small spaces. Not fully claustrophobic, but the thought of being locked in a small space heightened fear for me.

Perhaps it didn't bother Dorothy. Perhaps her fear had stemmed from the thought that whoever pushed her into the closet would return to harm her. With that thought, I looked around the closet, identifying a few items that could serve as weapons: the broom, mop, bucket, and some of the cleaning sprays or liquids. Would they have been enough to hold off an attacker? Would she have heard the attacker approaching and been ready for them?

That thought made me aware of the sounds I could hear. Both dogs were snuffling the floor.

Paw gave a low growl in his throat. Could he detect Bitsy's lingering scent? She had been in the closet with Dorothy.

Other sounds came to me. People talking. Clear conversation. An announcer speaking over the PA system. But Dorothy said she hadn't heard anything. Could I hear people because they were walking past the door? The night of the murder we were at the side entrance of the hall which was quite some ways away from the closet. And yet, we eventually heard Dorothy crying for help. Had she stayed quiet, fearing her attacker would come back? And, if so, why did she risk banging on the door if she couldn't hear us?

I wondered how clear it would be to hear sounds from in the closet when the hall was quieter. Right now, I couldn't test my theory, and I needed to get out of here. I went to the door and began banging on it and yelling for help.

Paw and Samuel began barking as well.

A man's voice on the other side of the door called, "We hear you!" Someone tried turning the knob, but it wouldn't budge. "This door is locked. Do you know where the key is?"

"No. I don't!"

"It's okay. You don't have to shout. I can hear you clearly. My friend is going to find a hotel employee, and we'll get you out."

I sighed with relief. Using my normal voice, I said, "Okay. Thank you." I patted both dogs who quieted.

"No problem."

I was coming to treasure his voice.

He asked, "Are you involved in the dog show? I hear you have a dog or two with you."

I chuckled. "Hard to miss, aren't they?"

He laughed.

"We were in the Saint Bernard competition, but we lost. My name is Clarissa."

Both dogs barked.

He laughed again. "Name's Steve. I show cairn terriers. Do you have two Saints in there with you?"

"No. One is my Saint Bernard. His name is Paw. Plus, I have a mastiff whose name is Samuel."

"Paw. I bet I can guess how he got that name."

I laughed.

"Samuel. I know a mastiff by that name. He belongs to Gerald Hoffman. I should say belonged." He lowered his voice. "He's the guy who was murdered."

"Same dog. My friends and I are taking care of him. My friend, Shelbee, is a pet sitter. She has a natural way with animals, and the mastiff was heartbroken when Hoffman died."

"Shelbee Van Vight?"

"Yes. Do you know her?"

"Sure. Everybody knows Shelbee. She's amazing. She helped me solve a problem I had with Tyler, my top cairn terrier."

"That's Shelbee all right."

Steve asked, "How long have you been competing?"

My first thought was that I never competed with Shelbee then I realized he meant the dog shows. It dawned on me that he was making conversation to keep me calm until someone came with the keys.

"This is our first competition. How about you?"

"We've been competing for five years." I could hear the smile in his voice. "I fell in love with cairns when I met my first one as a child. They have such intelligent and soulful eyes."

My legs were getting tired standing in one place, so I sat down. "Have you won many competitions?"

"Some, but for me, it's more about showing off the breed. I want others to see how beautiful and accomplished cairns can be." He chuckled again. "Plus, I do love it when we win."

I laughed. "I can only imagine winning." I decided I might as well do a little investigating while I locked in this closet. Steve had been in the shows for several years. Perhaps he could enlighten me on some of our suspects.

"Are most of the show owners like you? I mean do they love the breed and want to display their best qualities or are they super competitive and only here to win?"

"I think most are like me. Winning is a great feeling, but every dog is a winner to his owner. The ribbons and trophies are nice, but most of us I believe just love our breeds."

"But are there some who only compete to win at any cost?"

His voice hardened. "I would never condone that. I hope you aren't here only to win." He sounded both angry and a little disappointed in me.

"No. I'm not, but I have heard of others who are competing at any cost. It made me wonder if that had anything to do with Hoffman's death."

"I don't know. Fortunately, I didn't have much contact with the guy, but it was well-known that he was difficult to get along with." His voice faded as if he had moved away from the door then returned to its previous strength. "Here comes my friend. We'll have you out in a minute."

I heard him ask, "Where's the key?"

A new male voice said, "It's coming. It'll probably be another fifteen minutes."

Steve huffed. "What! That's ridiculous."

The new man responded, "I know. I know. They only have one key to this closet, held by the manager."

Steve's voice rose. "Only one key?"

"Yeah. Seems stupid to me."

Steve griped, "Then get the manager's key."

"Easy buddy. I'm trying, but the manager has the key on him, and he is trapped in the elevator between floors. Hotel maintenance is busily working to get him out, but they told me it would be a little while longer."

Steve cursed. "My apologies, Clarissa. It seems we will have to wait a while longer. Let me introduce you to my buddy, Jim."

I called through the door, "Hi, Jim."

Paw and Samuel woofed their greetings.

"Hi, Clarissa. Sounds like you have some company in there."

"I do. Paw is my Saint Bernard, and Samuel was Hoffman's mastiff."

Jim whistled. "That was a shock. His murder I mean. Not that the guy was well liked but murder? Never thought something like that would happen at a dog show."

Here was my chance to get more information. "Did you know him?"

"Not really. I talked to him once at a show. He was a

brusque sort of guy. All business with the show. I don't show dogs, so he didn't pay much attention to me which was a good thing. I've seen him disdainfully dismiss his weak competition and argue with his top competitors."

"Anyone, in particular, he argued with?" I felt something wet and sticky on my legs and looked down to see that both dogs had drooled on me. Both Saints and mastiffs have a habit of drooling a lot. Both dogs had a puddle of drool on the floor as well.

I stood up to reach for a roll of paper towels on one of the shelves while Jim answered me.

"It varied with whoever looked to be the strongest competition at any given show. A few dog owners always seemed to be the top competitors. Dorothy and her husband won more often than not. You know Dorothy, right?"

I reached up for a roll of paper towels while answering him. "Yes." *Why does it seem that the things I need are stored on the top shelf?* This was the bane of everyone who was short.

Jim was continuing to talk. "Hoffman and Fred Hawkins were always trying to beat the other one to a show win. I've seen Dorothy's husband and Hoffman in violent verbal confrontations in the past. Of course, her husband died about a year ago."

I already knew this which is why I wasn't paying attention to him. Instead, I was standing on tiptoe using my fingertips to edge the roll of towels out far enough to grab. Finally, I managed enough of a hold on them to pull them down.

Ow!

Something clunked me on the head and clattered to the floor. I rubbed my head and looked down to see what had hit me. A roll of toilet paper lay on the floor.

Paw jumped up to sniff at it then woofed, eager to play with it.

Both men spoke at the same time.

"What's wrong?"

"Everything okay?"

I bent to retrieve the roll before Paw nosed it all over the floor. "We're fine."

Steve's voice held concern. "What happened?"

"A roll of toilet paper fell on my head."

Silence met my answer for a few moments.

Jim laughed. "How did that happen?"

"The dogs were drooling, and I needed something to wipe it up. The toilet paper must have been stuck to the roll of paper towels and caught on them as I pulled down the towels. Why is it that everything I need to reach is on the top shelf?"

I could hear the amusement in Jim's voice. "You must be a short person because it would be ideal on a high shelf for a tall person to reach."

"True."

Outside I heard loud voices approaching the closet.

The voice of Mr. Jackson, the hotel manager, was

demanding, "Find out what happened to those keys and get that elevator working again."

I could hear the hotel manager's strident voice outside. "All right. I'm here. Does somebody want to tell me what is going on? Who's trapped in the closet?"

Steve growled. "Just get the door open."

Mr. Jackson huffed.

I heard the key inserted in the lock, a click, and the door swung open. Three men stood outside. Mr. Jackson wore a scowl while the other two men smiled broadly. One had wavy brown hair with sun highlights and forest-green eyes. The other had auburn hair and brilliant blue eyes. Both men were tall and had athletic builds.

The brown-haired man on my left spoke. "Nice to put a face to the voice." This was Steve. To my right, Jim winked at me.

The manager asked with indignation, "How did you get locked there? Did you kick the wedge away?"

Steve scowled. "What wedge?"

"The wooden wedge we use to prop the door."

Steve was examining the door lock. Distractedly, he asked, "Why do you need a wedge to block the door?" He paused. "Hey," he said, turning to the manager, "Why do you have a closet that locks and unlocks with a key? Most closets have a lock on only one side."

Jim ventured, "Let me guess. The construction crew gave you the wrong door and to save money you kept it this way."

The hotel manager's shoulders slumped. "It's only

been in two weeks. We're waiting for the contractor to come back and replace it."

Jim nodded. "That's why you only have one key."

Steve shook his head. "And why you are using a wooden wedge to prop the door open during the dog show. That way the fanciers have access and don't run to you to open it every few minutes."

A deep male voice responded, "That's true."

In my focus on the manager, I hadn't heard the approach of more people.

The deep voice belonged to a tall, coffee-skinned man in a hotel uniform. Behind him and to the side stood Bruce. Behind Bruce stood Shelbee and Jac.

Both dogs had followed me out of the closet, and Samuel now lunged for Shelbee, tail wagging.

The hotel security guard neatly stepped out of his way as did Bruce.

The manager glanced at his head of security. "Is there a problem?"

"Yes, sir. You asked me to check if any keys are missing. I've discovered a set of maid's keys have disappeared. Ms. Magee swears she had them yesterday, but today she can't find them."

The manager asked, "Did she lose them?"

The guard shook his head. "No, sir, I don't believe so. She is a conscientious worker. I have instigated a search for the missing keys. Do you want me to inform Detective Gibbons?"

Mr. Jackson paled. "No. I'll inform her."

MASTIFFS, MYSTERY, AND MURDER

Steve asked, "The maid's keys don't open the closet?"

Mr. Jackson crossed his arms. "No. As I said, I have the only key to the closet. Now, if you'll excuse us." He motioned for the guard to follow him.

The guard nodded to us, and they walked away.

I scanned the floor.

Bruce put his arm around me. "What are you looking for?"

"The wooden wedge. When the dogs and I entered the closet, the door was propped open. I swear I didn't kick it out of the way, nor did the dogs."

Bruce frowned. "Somebody locked you in the closet?"

"It appears that way."

Steve, Jim, Jac, and Shelbee began searching the floor, which was easy as most of the crowd had thinned out.

The dogs were sitting at our feet.

Samuel observed Shelbee with his head cocked to the side. He woofed.

Paw woofed back.

The dogs stared into each other's eyes.

Both stood up and trotted over to a nearby stall.

Samuel grasped something in his mouth, then trotted back, Paw by his side.

He placed the object at my feet.

Bruce bent down and picked it up. He held it up for us to see. It was a piece of wood, shaped into a wedge, just the right size to prop under a door. "The wedge, I presume."

Shelbee nodded. "Looks like it."

CHAPTER 19

Over the PA system, the announcer said, "Five minutes to Best in Show."

Shelbee tugged on Samuel's leash, saying, "We better hurry if we want to see it."

I nudged Bruce. "What do we do with the wedge?"

"I'll hold onto it and show it to Sergeant Bull after Best in Show."

We headed as a group over to the show ring.

I introduced my friends. "Steve, Jim, these are my friends. Shelbee, Jac, Bruce, this is Steve and Jim."

Jim smiled at Jac in appreciation.

She returned the smile with one of her own. Hmm. A new romance?

Steve smiled at Shelbee. "I've heard lots of good things about you from my fellow fanciers."

Shelbee blushed. "Thank you."

As we walked to the ring, Steve, who was walking on my left, asked, "Isn't Colby Matt Monroe's girlfriend?"

Bruce was on my right while Paw walked in front of us, tugging me along. Up ahead Shelbee led the way with Samuel, who eagerly pulled her forward. Jim walked next to Jac, just in front of us.

Bruce put his arm around my shoulders. "She is."

I sighed with a mix of exasperation and delight. I loved that he was protective, but I was irritated with his jealousy of other men near me.

Bruce questioned Steve. "Why do you ask?"

"It's just that Clarissa asked me who Hoffman argued with and I saw Matt arguing with him yesterday."

I walked fast to keep up with both men. "We saw that. Bruce had to step between them. I was afraid they would start fighting amongst all the spectators in the aisle."

Steve raised his eyebrow. "There were no spectators. This was after the show ended for the day. Matt and Hoffman were in the stairwell. They were yelling at each other at full volume. Hoffman accused Matt of complaining to the officials about him. Matt was accusing him of cheating. Both men glared at me as I hurried past them to the lobby."

My eyes widened. "Wow! That makes two fights Matt had with Hoffman."

Bruce hugged me closer. "Matt never mentioned that fight. He claimed to have stayed in his room the whole time." He checked his watch. "We need to question him and Colby again."

Steve nodded thoughtfully. "You'll have to wait until the competition is over."

We entered the ring. Three of the former group rings were combined into one for the Best in Show competition. Bleacher seating surrounded the ring on all four sides with an opening for the entrance and between each set of bleachers. The seats were packed.

We found room to squeeze our group in at the top of the viewing platform. Below us, I saw Alex and Rachel sitting together. They were talking to a set of older women in brightly-colored clothes. Matt sat in the first row directly below them. Across the ring, Judge Gray and Sal were sitting together, talking to several other dog owners that I had seen in my travels through the events hall.

A movement caught my eye, and I turned my head. Detective Gibbons stood in one of the openings with Sergeant Bull and the hotel manager. The manager was wildly gesticulating as he spoke with her. His actions appeared to be a bit desperate, but I was too far away to hear their conversation.

The detective gave a brief nod, and the manager seemed to relax as he lowered his hands to his sides. He walked toward the center of the ring.

Shelbee sat up straighter, trying to peer around the woman in front of her. "Ooh. They got Judith Carson to judge."

I assumed Shelbee was referring to the tall woman in the gray suit standing at the edge of the inner ring. She was studying a notebook held in her hands while three helpers waited on her directions.

Jac cocked her head to the side to catch what Shelbee was saying. "Is that important?"

The arena was loud, and Jac sat two seats down from Shelbee. Jim had sat between my friends.

Nevertheless, Shelbee has phenomenal hearing. "Yes, it is. Judge Carson is one of the most influential judges in the dog show realm. Her opinion is highly respected. Any owner would be proud to be judged by her. And to win under her judging would be a career highlight."

Paw, who couldn't see for all the people in front of us, sighed and settled across my feet.

Samuel, who had already stretched across Shelbee and Steve's feet, snuffled in agreement.

They weren't impressed with the judge.

I studied Judge Carson. Her dark brown hair had a few gray strands beginning to show. She had her hair pulled up into a bun at the back of her head. Her posture was ramrod straight giving the impression of a general about to go to battle. This harsh effect was softened by her kind brown eyes and the smile she directed toward the competitors as they lined up for the judging.

There were eight competitors in the Best in Show. They represented the seven working groups. The additional competitor was due to the tie in the Toy Group. These two were Dorothy and her Pomeranian, Bitsy, and Colby and Matt's Chihuahua, Lila. The remaining competitors included Ina and her mastiff, Max, representing the Working Group and an Irish setter competing for the Sporting Group. The final competitors included a beagle (Hound Group), a West Highland White (Terrier Group), a poodle (Non-Sporting Group), and a Border collie who represented the Herding Group.

I continued to observe the ring. "I hope Ina wins." I thought she truly deserved Best in Show.

Steve dashed my hopes. "The poodle is going to be hard to beat."

Shelbee nodded her agreement.

Bruce asked the question I was thinking. "Why?"

Steve answered, "There are certain breeds of dogs who have won more competitions than other breeds. In fact, many breeds have never won Best in Show."

Shelbee added, "Poodles are one of the top breeds."

I huffed. "That hardly seems fair."

Shelbee and Steve both shrugged. Shelbee said, "It's the way it is."

I was beginning to dislike this competition before it even began.

The dogs and their owners were now lined up. Dorothy was first with Bitsy followed by Colby and Lila. Ina came next. Beside her, a tall, thin woman with a pinched expression held the leash of the terrier. Continuing down the line, the next competitor was the poodle who stood in place like she was a star. Oddly enough, her owner reminded me of a certain movie star. I wondered if the poodle's name was Rocky. The Border collie was sixth in line standing next to a young woman with mocha skin and a huge smile. The Irish setter stood half as tall as the middle-aged man who was dressed in a tan suit. He smiled fondly down at his dog. Finally, the beagle was at the end of the line staring intently at the judge while his towering owner stood straight to his full height, well over six feet tall.

Steve observed me studying the beagle. "He knows the judge because he boards with her when his owner travels." That explained the beagle's eager expression.

"Wouldn't that cause a conflict of interest?"

"Sometimes." Steve shrugged. "Judge Carson is considered above reproach."

"She's that highly respected?"

Steve nodded.

The hotel manager, Mr. Jackson, reached the center of the ring. He addressed the spectators. "Welcome everyone." A sharp screech echoed from his microphone.

I winced, and Paw and Samuel lifted their heads at the noise.

The competing dogs stood still ignoring the sound while several of the human participants visibly cringed.

"The Haliburton is proud to present the final competition: Best in Show." He gestured with his free hand toward the line-up of competitors. "We are all pleased that you could join us in celebrating these fine champions." He continued talking, introducing the dogs and their owners, or handlers, as the case may be.

I had learned from Shelbee that many owners would hire a professional dog handler to show their dog in the ring. While the manager continued talking, two women sitting in front of me were discussing using handlers.

The woman with red hair pointed at the line-up of dogs. "Look. There are two handlers in the show."

Her friend shook her head. "No, there are not. The beagle's owner is using a handler. I see him sitting in the front row down there." She pointed down in front of our bleachers. "But you can't count Colby."

The red-haired woman huffed. "Why not?"

Her friend nudged her. "Because Colby is Matt Monroe's girlfriend. She's practically family. That don't count."

Her friend huffed.

I tuned them out and concentrated on the manager. He finished his introductions of the competitors and moved on to introduce Judge Carson, who nodded to the crowd. He then handed the microphone over to another distinguished-looking man with salt and pepper hair who would give brief commentary as the judging commenced.

Judge Carson walked over to a raised platform and gestured for Dorothy to bring Bitsy forward.

Each step smooth as silk, they approached the platform where Dorothy lifted Bitsy and placed her on the pedestal. Both had been through this routine many times, and it showed in their ease with each other and the judge. Bitsy's stance was perfect, and she patiently allowed Judge Carson to run her hands over her fur.

The commentator, in a reserved voice, explained the

standards in Pomeranian breeds. "The judge is comparing this dog against those standards."

Was Bitsy the epitome of her breed? She did behave beautifully.

Satisfied, the judge motioned for Dorothy to take Bitsy for a short walk then a quick run to check her gait. How Bitsy moved was important although perhaps not as discernible as how the larger dogs moved.

Bitsy's little feet flew over the ground as she looked up happily at Dorothy.

The judge motioned Dorothy to a stop and knelt to Bitsy's level.

I could see a slight smile on the judge's face. A good indication since the judge needed to maintain a reserved demeanor throughout the judging to avoid favoritism.

Judge Carson motioned Dorothy and Bitsy back to the line-up and nodded for Colby and Lila to step forward.

Colby glided to the pedestal as Lila walked with confidence. Her mannerisms said that she'd been here before and loved the attention. Colby lifted Lila onto the pedestal and stepped back.

Judge Carson examined Lila who stood patiently as the judge's hands caressed her. The judge nodded and gestured to Colby to do the same walk and run as Dorothy. Lila was adorable running.

I just wanted to pick her up and hug her.

Colby smoothly walked alongside Lila showing off the little dog's gait to its best advantage.

Steve whispered to Shelbee, "Colby knows how to make Lila look good."

Shelbee nodded once in agreement.

The commentator was continuing his quiet observations about Chihuahua breed characteristics, but I stopped listening.

Judge Carson knelt to Lila. A quick look then she motioned Colby and Lila back in line. No emotion showed on her face.

I hoped that wasn't a bad sign.

Ina was next. The pedestal had been removed allowing more room for the large dogs. I wondered if they would bring it back for the beagle and West Highland White.

Ina and Max stepped forward. Ina was wearing a lovely rose-colored dress with a flared skirt that allowed ease of movement while Max wore a collar and leash of the same color.

I hadn't considered coordinating an owner's outfit to the dog's collar. As Judge Carson examined Max, I glanced at the other participants.

Dorothy, too, was coordinated with Bitsy in colors of black and gold.

Colby was wearing a dress suit in a dark blue which coordinated with Lila.

Not everyone chose to coordinate though. The pinch-faced terrier woman wore all gray while the terrier's collar was bright red which drew the eye to the dog's lovely white fur. The young woman who was showing the Border collie was wearing a white blouse with a conservative black skirt. These colors coordinated with the collie's black and white fur but not its purple collar and leash. None of the men coordinated their clothes with their dogs' collars. They all wore conservative suits in tan, gray, or black while the various collars worn were in a range of colors.

Judge Carson had finished examining Max when I refocused on the judging.

Ina was now fast walking her mastiff.

Once again, I was in awe of her ease and fluid motion. She agilely kept pace with her much larger dog. I looked down at Paw who was napping. How lovely it would be to run with him with such ease instead of being nearly dragged in his wake.

I wasn't the only one who noticed the beauty of Ina and Max in motion. Many heads in the audience were nodding in approval. We, the audience, had been instructed not to clap or make loud noises while the competition was progressing. This was to keep the dogs calm and avoid influencing the outcome.

Ina finished walking Max and stood for one final exam by Judge Carson.

As she was motioned back to her place in line, I felt the urge to clap. I glanced down to where Alex sat and saw that he was covering his mouth with his hand to prevent himself from exclaiming his approval. We both restrained our impulses, and I refocused on the competition.

I must admit to losing some interest in the rest of the competition once the dogs I knew had been judged.

Shelbee and Steve continued to watch in rapt attention as Jim was pointing out something to Jac.

I glanced to Bruce on my left. He wasn't watching the show at all but was scanning the crowd, tensed for trouble.

It hadn't occurred to me that there would be trouble during the show. I had assumed that Hoffman had been behind the other interruption and that the killer wouldn't attack in so open a venue. Of course, Bruce's instincts run to being on alert as he was a former cop before becoming a private detective. I noticed his eyes had settled on the area where Detective Gibbons had been standing.

I turned my head to the right and observed that three more police officers had joined her and Sergeant Bull. They stood watching the show, waiting for Detective Gibbons's orders. It dawned on me that she may have been waiting for the show to end.

Sergeant Bull occasionally glanced toward Matt sitting at the bottom of our bleachers. Bull glanced up at where Bruce and I sat and gave an almost imperceptible nod to Bruce.

I heard Bruce curse under his breath and turned to see him nod back.

He turned his head toward me and stared into my eyes then rubbed his wrist.

Puzzled, I frowned.

He breathed one word, "Cuffs."

My expression must have registered surprise and a trace of annoyance for he shrugged his shoulders. So the detective was ready to make an arrest. She was waiting for the end of the show.

I turned my head back toward the detective. As I did so, I saw the young woman with the Border collie walking her dog. I watched a moment then turned to observe Detective Gibbons and was surprised once again.

She, too, had a rapt attention on her face as she followed the progress of the Border collie. Odd.

I thought that she didn't like dogs.

The commentator concluded his remarks as the judge released the Border collie back to the line-up. That left the Irish setter and the beagle.

I hadn't paid much attention when the West Highland White and the poodle had been judged. My stomach growled as the Irish setter stepped forward to be judged. I had missed lunch while I was trapped in the supply closet.

Shelbee handed me a protein bar, smiled, and winked. She and Jac knew how much I liked to snack.

I tore open the wrapper and took a big bite. Mm. Delicious.

Both dogs raised their heads and began to wag their tails at the sound of the wrapper tearing.

I didn't trust giving them a taste, fearing that the bar contained something dangerous to dogs.

Bruce reached out with dog biscuits for Paw and

Samuel. He was learning how to be a prepared dog owner.

Both dogs graciously accepted their treat and crunched away. It didn't take long for them to devour their biscuits or for me to devour the protein bar.

The Irish setter was finished, and the beagle stepped up. The beagle's alert gaze centered on Judge Carson.

I was amazed how calmly the beagle stood for her, considering that he boarded with her. I had expected him to show some sign of recognition, but he was totally professional.

A quick walk with a second exam and the beagle was done.

Now everyone waited while the judge walked up and down the line-up and deliberated.

She returned to her group of helpers and wrote in her notebook, then instructed the competitors to make a circuit of the area at a slow walk. She watched them progress a short way and then finished her notes.

The owners and dogs finished the circuit and halted, turning to face Judge Carson who went to stand several feet in front of them.

She began pulling them out one at a time and lining them up.

Dorothy and Bitsy were the first to be pulled out.

Colby and Lila were next and were placed to Dorothy's left.

Then came the poodle followed by the Border collie.

Next was the beagle then the West Highland terrier and the Irish setter.

That left Ina standing by herself in the original line-up.

I was heartbroken, interpreting this to mean that Ina was last.

Beside me, Steve whispered to no one in particular, "Watch for it."

Shelbee muttered "mmhmm" in response.

Both knew, or suspected, something that I didn't.

The judge motioned to Ina and placed her to Dorothy's right.

She stood back and observed then began counting off. "One." She motioned to Ina. "Two." She motioned to Dorothy and Bitsy. She continued down the line to the Irish setter who was number eight and last.

The commentator had stepped to the judge's side.

She took his microphone. "Ladies and Gentlemen. This year's Best in Show." She motioned toward Ina. "The mastiff, Max, with his owner Ina Holmes."

CHAPTER 20

*A*pplause erupted from the bleachers.

Alex whistled and catcalled and rushed down to Ina who was gratefully accepting Judge Carson's compliments and the winning trophy.

I glanced at Dorothy whose expression changed from shock to disappointment to fury. I blinked. Fury? I refocused on her face to find she had plastered on a grim smile as she hugged Bitsy in her arms.

Had I really seen fury on her face? I glanced at Colby who was valiantly trying to hold back tears.

She had Lila cradled in her arms and was accepting the judge's compliments with a watery smile.

The judge placed a reassuring hand on Colby's shoulder then advanced down the line.

Matt stepped up to Colby and enveloped her and Lila in a big hug.

Across the arena, I saw Judge Gray smile, tip his head toward me, and beam down at Ina.

Sal had turned in his seat and was talking to someone sitting behind him.

The bleachers on our side were emptying as fellow dog owners, and spectators, ventured out to congratulate the winner. Others headed out of the ring, preparing to return to their dogs and begin packing up.

Now is when we needed to solve our case.

Jac, Jim, Shelbee, and Steve stood up and walked out of our aisle, Samuel leading Shelbee.

She maneuvered him through the tight aisle, saying, "That was fantastic judging. I'm so glad Ina won, but I do feel sorry for Dorothy."

Jac paused, causing Jim to stop short or risk running into her from behind. "Why?"

Bruce and I had stood up as well and were following behind Steve.

Paw impatiently began tugging on his leash. He wanted more space to move.

Steve turned to Jac. "This is likely Dorothy's last show." He stepped into the main aisle and began to descend to the arena floor. "Bitsy has been competing for a while. Show dogs only compete so long."

Maybe that explained Dorothy's expression that I had glimpsed. Certainly losing her last competition could make her angry.

Jim spoke over his shoulder. "She's not the only one. This was Lila's last show too."

I was shocked. "Really? I thought she was still young."

"Not as young as she would appear." Jim handed Jac down the last step to the arena floor.

Steve helped Shelbee as well. "Lila will be breeding for a while, but her competition days are over."

No wonder Colby had been in tears.

I sympathized with her and Lila. Then I looked down at Paw and realized that being loved and well-cared for was the most important thing.

Both Bitsy and Lila had good, loving homes.

Bruce helped me down the last step and onto the crowded floor. Being tall, he could see much farther than I could. "Detective Gibbons and her officers are advancing through the crowd toward the competitors." He snorted. "The hotel manager is following in their wake, wringing his hands. Guess a police arrest isn't good for business."

Jim commented over his shoulder. "Better an arrest than an unsolved murder."

I wondered if the manager had found out who had taken the maid's keys.

Paw was tugging on his leash again. People were pressing on all sides, upsetting him.

A blonde-haired woman passed me, saying to her brunette friend, "I love the way they coordinate their colors."

I stopped in my tracks, struck by a memory.

Paw looked back at me in irritation. He wanted to

SANDRA BAUBLITZ

move, so he gave a jerk on the leash, pulling me from my thoughts.

I started walking again. "Okay. We'll go."

Bruce remained focused on the detective. "She's reached the competitors."

Shelbee gasped, "I don't believe it."

All I could see were the backs of people walking in front of me. "What?" It was frustrating being short sometimes.

Bruce grimaced. "She's arresting Colby."

I pushed forward, trying to get closer to the detective. "She's making a mistake." I was convinced I knew who had murdered Hoffman.

Bruce looked down at me. "You know who did it."

"Yes, I think it's …"

The crowd surged toward me, separating me from Bruce and the others.

"… Dorothy."

I was pushed along, back toward the ring entrance, barely able to stand, unable to find Bruce.

People pushed and prodded in their quest to get out of the hall.

Suddenly, a strong arm clasped my shoulders.

I turned, expecting to see Bruce's reassuring expression.

To my dismay, Dorothy held me close to her. She shoved Bitsy into my arms. "Hold onto her, dear. Come on, let's get out of here."

Dorothy pushed and shoved people out of her way.

She cleared a path through the crowd, like a scythe through wheat.

Her arm remained clasped around my shoulders once we left the crowd as she guided me to her stall.

She urged me into a chair. "Here, dear. Sit down and hold Bitsy. That was quite an ordeal."

Bitsy knelt on my lap, looking like a powder puff. Her black and gold collar gleamed from the overhead lighting.

I cradled her, worrying my lower lip. I had to find Bruce.

Dorothy busied herself with the teapot. "What you need is a nice cup of tea. I hope you don't mind, but I could use some company." She drew a tissue from her pocket and wiped her eyes.

I sighed, wondering how was I going to get away from Dorothy. "I'm so sorry that you and Bitsy didn't win." I shifted in my chair, trying to find a way to rid myself of her.

She sighed. "Thank you, dear. I admit I am deeply disappointed." She sniffled again and reached for a tissue in her pocket. "I feel I've failed Bitsy and Fred."

It took me a few seconds to understand that she was referring to her deceased husband. "I'm sure he would be proud of you and Bitsy. We can't always win." I looked down at the sweet Pomeranian sitting in my lap. "Bitsy loves you and wouldn't want you to be sad."

"Yes. I suppose you are right. Bitsy loves to show, but she would forgive me. Sadly, my husband wouldn't, nor should he." She sighed. "I know you mean well dear, but winning *is* everything. I don't mean for you to feel bad about your loss. You have to understand, Fred and I have been - she corrected herself - had been competing and breeding for years. We were, and still are, the best. Bitsy should have won this competition. She is the superior animal!"

I was stunned. I knew Dorothy took competing seriously, but I never suspected that she believed her abilities superior to all the rest of us.

From what I had observed about the other owners, most were philosophical about winning and losing. They accepted that losses occurred and you moved on.

Dorothy handed me a cup of tea. "Here, dear. Have some tea."

I balanced the teacup on one palm. "I don't mean to question your opinion, but I thought Ina did a great job in the competition."

Dorothy snorted. "She only won because the judges felt sorry for her. My guess is that she bought off somebody."

I was shocked at Dorothy's vitriol. I prodded her, my inner sleuth hoping to get Dorothy to confess. "Has Ina caused trouble for you, Dorothy?"

She motioned to my cup. "Drink your tea, dear, and I'll tell you."

I raised the cup to my lips, but it was too hot. I blew on it. "I need to let it cool."

She frowned, then put on a smile. "Ina has been known to disrupt competition in the ring."

I blew on my tea again. "How?"

Dorothy handed me a spoon, motioning to the tea. "Stir it." She sighed. "I've heard Ina released a dog in the ring in the past."

"But the dog that got loose in the ring during her competition could have caused Ina's dog to lose."

Dorothy narrowed her eyes at me, her voice turning cold. "And what do you know about it?"

"I don't. I only know that the dog messed up Rachel's performance instead of Ina's."

"That was a mistake."

My eyes widened. Did she just confess?

"Don't look so innocent. I know you, and your detective boyfriend, have been nosing around asking questions. All worried about what happened to Lyon Connors." She grumbled. "He was a sorry no good excuse for a friend. Caused more trouble than a little. To think my Fred helped him to win several competitions. What does he do in return? Tries to stab us in the back, that's what."

Before I could curb my tongue, I asked, "Did you kill him?"

She stared at me a long while.

I expected her to deny it and throw me out of her stall.

Instead, she sneered. "Pretty smart, aren't you? Yes, I

killed him. Always did say a cup of tea solved everything. Too many times he tried his dirty tricks on us and won competitions. Someone had to stop him. My poor husband couldn't do it anymore, so I took care of the problem." She smirked. "And I would have taken care of Ina if that young Spaniard hadn't been at her side all the time."

I gasped.

Dorothy was the murderer.

"Oh, don't look so shocked."

I had to get away from her. "Did you kill your husband?"

"I most certainly did not!" She sounded genuinely affronted at my question. "I loved him dearly. He was a good man."

I couldn't agree with her. "But you did kill Hoffman and try to blame the death on Colby."

She grimaced. "He should have kept his nose out of things. No one liked him. He was a real grump. To think that he was going to complain to the judges about that choker collar. Just because my husband used to use it, doesn't mean I would anymore." She looked down and cooed at Bitsy. "Certainly not on my little sweetkins. I told Fred I wouldn't stand for him using it anymore and he stopped. So I brought it along and slipped it into a competitor's luggage then set the officials on him. It wasn't going to be used on the dog. But Hoffman saw me do it and was suddenly going to get high and mighty with morals. Can you imagine?

"I met Hoffman to 'discuss' with him why he shouldn't

go to the officials. There was no convincing him not to turn me in. We argued, and I pushed him. He laughed at me when he fell into those boxes and said he would see me out of the competition. We had to win this competition. Bitsy isn't young anymore. He turned his back on me, and I saw red. I grabbed that shovel and bashed him on the head. To be sure he was dead, I took the choker collar from his hands and wrapped it around his neck."

I think she honestly believed that I would agree with her.

"But how did you kill him if you were locked in the closet?"

She laughed in delight. "I locked myself in the closet after I killed him." She narrowed her eyes again. "And you would still be in there, too, if not for those two interfering young men."

My mouth dropped open.

She laughed. "Shocked, are you? It was easy to kick that prop away and slam the door. It's a shame you got out though."

I had to get away from her. I picked up Bitsy, planning to stand when I glanced down at my teacup, then to Dorothy.

She wore a small smile.

I gulped, relieved I hadn't taken a sip. "The tea is poisoned, isn't it?"

She smirked. "Of course, I always say a good cup of tea solves anything."

She pulled a gun from the folds of her skirt and aimed

it at me. "Since you won't drink the tea, we'll have to resort to Plan B. Get up!"

I lunged, tossing the tea at her.

Bitsy jumped from my arms, tripping me as I stumbled over her.

Dorothy slammed the barrel of the gun into my side. "Don't move!"

I froze.

CHAPTER 21

*C*almly, she said, "You are going to escort me out of here, my dear."

"You won't get away with this."

She smiled. "I already have. Colby has been arrested, and your boyfriend will return to find you gone. Now pick up Bitsy and cuddle her. I don't want my sweetheart alarmed."

She held onto my left arm. It became apparent that she intended to leave all her stuff behind. "You are my insurance out of here," she murmured into my ear. "Make a move to alert anyone, and I'll put a bullet into them."

I believed her.

She marched me out of the stall. Fortunately, in the time I had been talking with Dorothy, the aisle had emptied out of most of the owners and their dogs. We began walking down the aisle toward the main entrance.

Bitsy was surprisingly calm and relaxed in my arms.

Dorothy stayed close by me, keeping the gun tight against my side so that it wasn't visible to the few people we passed.

As we advanced down the aisle, I gazed from side to side desperately trying to think what to do next. I ran through my options, determining that I didn't have many left. Any move I made was sure to get a bullet in my side. I briefly contemplated throwing Bitsy from my arms but decided against that plan. I couldn't bring myself to harm the little Pomeranian, however, and I imagined Dorothy would be quick to shoot me for doing such a thing.

Oddly in her own twisted way, Dorothy did truly love her dogs, especially Bitsy. The only thing I could do to distract her was to talk to her.

"You lost your brush when you fought with Hoffman."

"Ah. That's where it was." She growled. "I was forced to use that horrible blue and white one the show provided. Disgraceful. You'd think they could purchase better quality."

Bruce and Detective Gibbons entered the aisle some yards in front of us.

Sergeant Bull and two officers followed them.

My heart rate sped up. I cherished the sight of Bruce, but I feared what Dorothy would do.

Bruce frowned when he saw us.

Detective Gibbons spoke. "Mrs. Hawkins, we need to speak with you." The detective hadn't grasped the seriousness of the situation since the gun Dorothy held was hidden from view, but Bruce had.

"Let her go."

Dorothy moved the gun to the side of my neck. "Not a chance."

Detective Gibbons drew her weapon. "Put the gun down!"

Bruce crept forward while Dorothy's attention was on the detective.

Dorothy smirked at Gibbons. "No way. Clarissa and I are going to walk out of here - alone. You are going to step out of our way, or Clarissa is going to suffer the consequences."

"That's not going to happen, Mrs. Hawkins." The detective altered her tone to one of friendship. "There is no need to hold a gun on Ms. Hayes. We only wish to question you."

Dorothy laughed. "Drop your weapons and slide them over here and I might talk to you."

I doubted that.

Gibbons's officers looked to her for direction. She slowly lowered her weapon, nodding for her officers to do the same.

Bruce continued to creep closer.

Dorothy glanced at him, growling, "If you want Clarissa safe, you'll stay where you are."

Bruce halted.

Suddenly, chaos reigned.

Dorothy lifted her gun, aiming at Gibbons.

In the split second before Dorothy fired, Samuel

lunged from the side and knocked Gibbons to the ground.

The bullet missed Gibbons but hit the mastiff.

Bitsy jumped out of my arms, barking furiously.

Paw lunged at Dorothy, knocking the gun from her extended hand.

Something slammed into me.

I fell, landing on the carpeted aisle floor.

Dorothy landed partially on top of me, knocking the breath from me.

I looked up into the face of Ina's mastiff, Max, who had body slammed into Dorothy and me.

Bruce, Shelbee, and Jac pulled Dorothy off me.

Bruce helped me to stand. "Are you all right?"

I nodded.

Paw pushed through them to my side and woofed.

"Thank you, my dear friend." I bent down and hugged him in a fierce grip. Standing, I hugged Bruce.

He kissed me. "Don't ever scare me like that again."

"Trust me. I won't."

I thought of Samuel. Rushing over to where Detective Gibbons was being helped up by Sergeant Bull, I knelt by Samuel.

He lay on his side with Steve soothing him.

Sal pushed through us, medical bag in hand.

"Let me see him." He bent down and examined Samuel.

We all waited in tense silence.

Behind us, the officers were handcuffing Dorothy.

Sal looked up at us and smiled. "He's just been grazed by the bullet. Nothing serious. I can bandage him up, and he'll be fine."

Everyone let out a collective sigh of relief.

Gibbons stared at Samuel. "He saved my life."

She tentatively reached out to Samuel and pet his head.

He wore a big doggie grin with his tongue hanging out the side of his mouth.

Bitsy was biting the pants leg of one of the officers who was handcuffing Dorothy. "Get off." He was attempting to dislodge her by shaking his leg.

The second officer was distracted with holding onto Dorothy.

Dorothy scolded. "Don't you dare harm my little sweetheart."

Shelbee tried to grab Bitsy, who let go of the pants leg to snap at her.

Steve went to help her, but before he got there Ina's mastiff put his paw down gently onto Bitsy.

She growled, and Max growled back.

Bitsy relented.

Shelbee picked her up.

Dorothy spoke to Bitsy. "You're my good girl. I love you, sweetheart."

Bitsy wiggled to get to her.

"You be a good girl."

Bitsy started to whine.

Dorothy's sad tone was registering with her. Dorothy

looked up at Shelbee. "I trust you will take good care of her."

Shelbee nodded.

Dorothy sounded so sad it almost made me tearful, until I thought of the things she had done to win a dog show and my tears dried up.

"Detective?" One of the officers holding Dorothy called to Gibbons. "Where should we take her?"

Gibbons shook herself, withdrawing her hand from Samuel's back. Steel returned to her voice. "Take her to the station."

"Yes, ma'am. Ah, what about her dog?"

"Leave her with Ms. Van Vight."

The two officers escorted Dorothy away.

The detective motioned to me. "Ms. Hayes, please come with me. I need your statement." Gibbons turned and walked briskly away.

Bruce hugged me. "Go on."

I glanced back at the others as I walked away.

Ina and Alex were standing with Max.

Shelbee held Bitsy while Jac held Paw who wanted to follow me after once again saving my life. He was the best dog anyone could have.

I wanted to rush back to him and envelope him in a huge hug, but I knew I had to talk to Gibbons.

I followed the detective to the stall she had commandeered earlier.

The hall had nearly emptied. Our little scene hadn't attracted much attention.

Gibbons motioned for me to sit, so I pulled up a metal folding chair. "All right. Let's start with your statement. Tell me what happened."

"Where do you want me to start?"

"Begin with being locked in the closet."

I corralled my thoughts. "Paw pulled me to the closet. I went in to investigate. I know I didn't knock the prop out of the way."

"What did you hope to find?"

"I wondered why Dorothy wasn't found in the closet earlier. I assumed that it must have been soundproof, but when I was inside, I discovered that I could clearly hear voices on the other side of the door. Why did Dorothy wait to call for help?"

She listened patiently and didn't interrupt. "Did you suspect her at the time?"

I shook my head. "No. I assumed she had been too scared to call out."

She motioned for me to continue.

"Steve and Jim – do you know them?"

She nodded.

"They heard me and sent for the manager to get the key. Bruce and my friends joined us, and we went to watch Best in Show. After the competition was finished, I overheard a conversation between two women complimenting the matching outfits the owners wore."

She raised an eyebrow.

I smiled. "Their clothes match their dogs' collars. It triggered my memory. Dorothy's show colors are black and gold, just like the brush you found at the crime scene."

"The brush I have in evidence at the station?" Gibbons looked incredulous. "That is why you suspected Mrs. Hawkins?"

"Yes."

Gibbons scowled. "Why didn't you tell me about this?"

I huffed. "Because I was in the middle of a crowd of people that forced me away from Bruce. That's how Dorothy found me. She guided me out of the ring and to her stall. I chose to ask questions to determine if I was correct in assuming Dorothy was the murderer."

"Did she confess?"

I nodded. "She confessed to killing both Lyon Connors and Hoffman. She poisoned Connors. Check the teapot in her stall. She offered me tea, which I suspect is laced with poison.

"And she confessed to locking me in the closet. She indicated she planned to kill Ina Holmes as well, but couldn't get close to her. Ina's friend, Alex, was by her side all the time."

Gibbons called an officer to her. "Go to Mrs. Hawkins's stall and see if a teapot is there and full of tea. If so, have the crime scene guys bag it. That tea is evidence."

He nodded. "I'll tell them."

She turned back to me. "What about the attack on Matt Monroe? Was she the one responsible?"

"I don't know. She didn't confess to that. She did admit that she tried to put the blame on Colby."

Gibbons nodded. "I would like more evidence against her, however, based on her violent actions, we have a solid case. You are free to go now, Ms. Hayes. Leave your contact information with Officer Wells in case I need to question you further."

"Will you look into the death of Lyon Connors?"

"I'll notify the police in his district and suggest they re-examine the case."

I nodded. "Thank you."

"Ms. Hayes, can I ask you something?"

I was tempted to point out that she had just been asking questions but decided against it. I nodded in agreement instead.

"Is your dog always that loyal?"

I smiled broadly. "Yes, he is. Paw is the most loyal and loving dog I have ever had. He would do anything for me, and I would do anything for him."

She stared at me for a moment and nodded. "Thank you. You can go now."

I left, passing Bruce in the aisle.

He grasped my hand. "You okay?"

I squeezed his hand. "Yes."

Gibbons stepped out of the stall behind me. "Mr. Sever, I'll speak with you now."

Bruce followed her as I walked away.

The others were waiting for their turn to be questioned, so I returned to our hotel room to pack. By the time I finished, Bruce, Shelbee, and Jac had returned to the room.

Bruce hugged me and whispered, "Time to go. I've loaded Paw's things in the car."

"Do you think they'll look into Connors's death?"

He squeezed me. "If not, I will."

Shelbee held Bitsy while Samuel sat at her feet.

Paw was leaning heavily against me.

I tilted my head toward Bitsy and Samuel. "What will happen to them?"

Shelbee cuddled Bitsy. "Detective Gibbons has asked me to keep Bitsy and Samuel until she sorts everything out. Since Dorothy told me to protect her, Gibbons thinks she can stay with me."

"And Samuel?"

"The detective will let me know once she contacts Hoffman's family."

I felt sorry for both dogs. They had lost their owners and who knew what the law would decide. I looked down at Paw. I needed to make arrangements for him if anything ever happened to me. Of course, I knew that I would simply arrange to have Shelbee take over his care.

We grabbed up our bags, left the hotel, and headed home.

CHAPTER 22

*I*t had been several weeks since the dog show.
Paw continued to be his lovable, mischievous self. Just that morning, he had brought me my neighbor's well-chewed sneaker.

I had returned it and apologized profusely. Fortunately, I had an understanding neighbor who had a new puppy named Rex. He was a lovable mutt, and we both agreed that either dog could have been the culprit.

Bruce had been out of town working on the Connors case.

Bitsy was doing well in Shelbee's care, but Samuel had been retrieved by Hoffman's attorney. I hoped he was doing well.

I had stepped out on my front porch to sweep when Bruce pulled into the driveway.

He got out and walked up to me, embracing me in a huge hug.

"You must have good news."

He released me and smiled. "I do."

We went into the house where Paw stood up and slurped Bruce's face.

Bruce laughed. "Glad to see you, too, buddy."

I offered Bruce a drink, but he declined and took my hand, leading me to the sofa. We sat down, and Paw jumped up to join us. I gave him a gentle nudge to leave room for us. "What's the news?"

"Dorothy confessed to everything."

"Good, I'm glad to hear it."

"She admitted to killing Connors by drugging his tea. She told the police everything that she told you and more. Apparently, Hoffman wasn't the one who tried to drug Connors's dog. It was Dorothy's husband." Bruce shook his head at such folly. "It was just a dog show."

"True. They took competing too far." I looked at Paw.

His tongue lolled out in a happy smile. He certainly didn't miss the dog show.

I asked, "Did she confess to the attack on Matt?"

"She did. She claims she wasn't going to hurt Lila, just hide her so she couldn't compete. Matt interrupted her, so she hit him on the head. Lila bolted when she opened the latch on her cage. Dorothy was afraid someone would hear Lila barking, so she left the room."

"How did she get into his room? The missing maid's keys?"

Bruce nodded. "She stole them off the maid's cart. Gibbons found them in Dorothy's hotel room."

"What will happen to Bitsy?"

"Shelbee gets to keep her. Dorothy's wishes."

I smiled. "Good. Shelbee will love her."

Bruce agreed. "Samuel has a new home too."

"That's great! Paw misses him, though. Who adopted him?"

"Shelbee." He smiled at the delighted look on my face. "Paw will get to see Samuel as much as he wants."

"That is wonderful news!"

"None of Hoffman's extended family wanted the dog, so Shelbee gets to keep him. Did you know Samuel has a brother?"

"No, I didn't."

"His name is Clemens. He was the only other dog Hoffman had at the time of his murder. Fortunately, Hoffman had recently sold the last pups he had and their mother. Clemens was being taken care of by a pet sitter."

Bruce saw the worry on my face. "Don't start worrying. Clemens has a home now."

"That's wonderful. Who adopted him?"

With a huge grin, he said, "Detective Gibbons."

"But I thought she didn't like dogs?"

"Apparently, she changed her mind when Samuel tackled her to save her life. According to Sergeant Bull, the detective goes everywhere with Clemens, and both are devoted to each other."

I sighed with relief. I hadn't realized how worried I had been about the dogs. "I'm glad to hear it." I gazed adoringly at Paw. "Every dog should have a good home and a loyal friend."

Paw laid his head on my leg. He sighed contentedly.

Bruce put his arm around me. "Yes. And every man should have as wonderful a girlfriend as you."

My eyes watered at the heartfelt compliment. I reached up and caressed his jaw. "And every woman should have a strong, loving boyfriend."

Bruce leaned over and kissed me.

Sleuthing adventures could wait for another day.

REVIEW REQUEST

THANK you for reading. I truly appreciate your taking time from your busy day to read my novel. I know your time is limited, but could you do me a favor? Could you leave a review of this story? Reviews are an important part of a writer's marketing success.

Please see the *About the Author* page to contact Ms. Baublitz, and don't forget to sign up for the newsletter on her site to be the first to get updates on upcoming publications!

ABOUT THE AUTHOR

SANDRA Baublitz is a lover of all animals. She has always loved dogs and cats. A Dog Detective series originally began as a contest entry. Paw's creation was influenced by the Beethoven movies and the author's desire to own a Saint Bernard. The author never got the opportunity to own a St. Bernard and her current cats will not allow a new edition. Ms. Baublitz expresses her love of the breed by continuing to write about Clarissa and Paw and their mystery adventures. She hopes her readers enjoy reading them as much as she enjoys writing them.

Please don't forget to sign up for the newsletter on her site to be the first to get updates on upcoming publications!

sandrabaublitz.com

CPSIA information can be obtained
at www.ICGtesting.com
Printed in the USA
LVHW091524221120
672387LV00002B/277